ROAR, BULL, ROAR!

For our daughter Rosalind
who read it first, and for all the children and teachers
at Lydbury North Primary School.

With many thanks to Vera Fusek Peters
for language advice and great Czech meals over the years,
to Iva Kucharova for all the Czech colloquial expressions
and to Nikki Pugh for excellent legal advice!

Roar, Bull, Roar! copyright © Frances Lincoln Limited 2006
Text copyright © Andrew Fusek Peters and Polly Peters 2006
Illustrations copyright © Anke Weckmann

First published in Great Britain in 2006 and the USA in 2007
by Frances Lincoln Children's Books, 4 Torriano Mews,
Torriano Avenue, London NW5 2RZ
www.franceslincoln.com

Distributed in the USA by Publishers Group West

British Library Cataloguing in Publication Data
available on request

ISBN 10: 1-84507-520-X
ISBN 13: 978-1-84507-520-0

Printed and bound in Great Britain
by Bookmarque Ltd, Croydon, Surrey

1 3 5 7 9 8 6 4 2

Andrew Fusek Peters

Polly Peters

ROAR, BULL, ROAR!

Illustrated

by Anke Weckmann

F

FRANCES LINCOLN

CHILDREN'S BOOKS

Contents

A sudden change

Mrs Kleček screamed. Jan and Marie both woke with a start and their old Škoda screeched to a halt. In the light of the headlights, a huge bull thundered straight towards them down the narrow lane. Any second now, heavy hoofs would tear into the rusty car and its four passengers would be trampled. Marie could see red button eyes and nostrils pumping steam like chimneys. Instinctively their father put up his arms to shield himself. *Snap! Thud! Crunch!* The whole car shuddered as the bull pushed on past, scraping down the side and ripping away the wing mirror. Marie twisted round to see where it was going, but behind them lay only darkness. The bull had gone!

"That was fun! Can we do it again?" shrieked Jan, trying to cover the fact that a few seconds before he had been shaking with fear. Marie gave him a withering look. Mrs Kleček crossed herself and whispered a quick prayer of thanks as she nudged her husband to start the car. She muttered something about lazy farmers and open gates. But Marie could only think about the way the bull had stared at her: those burning eyes.

After a few hundred metres, the dirt track petered out and the car came to a stop for a second time.

"We are here!" said František, resting his arms on the steering wheel, exhausted after twenty-four hours of driving. Jan and Marie rubbed their eyes. 'Here' did not look so good. The headlights lit up an old cottage that might once have been white, but was now as grey as the weather they had driven through. Narrow metal windows, covered in peeling paint, stared blackly down at them. Their new home lay half a mile from the nearest town. There were no welcoming lights, just the grim darkness and the far-off barking of an angry dog.

"Ježiš-Maria!" sighed Mrs Kleček. 'Jesus-Maria' was about as rude as their mother got. She clicked her tongue in disapproval as František climbed out and ran through the driving rain to the shed where the agency had told him the key would be hanging.

Jan and Marie looked at each other and shrugged their shoulders. To think they had left their lovely house in Valašský Klobouky only yesterday morning! Germany had whizzed by in darkness and when they woke, they were gliding through the misty flat fields of France. Later, there was a ferry, which swallowed their car in its belly. The children had never seen the sea before. Their homeland, the Czech Republic, had no coast. It was a place of rivers and lakes and hot summers. But now it was cold and the waves of the

English Channel roared up and down. Their dinner of bread and smoked cheese had quickly vanished over the edge of the railings and they were thankful, but queasy, when they finally reached Dover.

However, the woman who checked their passports had spent ages asking their father questions, almost as if she didn't believe that "yes, he was a maths teacher and was invited to a proper job in a school in Shropshire," and, "no, he was not intending to seek asylum." Jan didn't understand, but he heard the icy tones under the woman's questions. Their father produced the teaching agency contract to prove he was not lying. The woman was not impressed. They had to wait in an ugly, strip-lit room for an hour while she made phone calls. At last she came back and reluctantly stamped their passports. With this cold welcome, the Klečeks drove into the twilight of a new country.

Jan and Marie sleepily began to think that England was just one big motorway. They stopped at a huge neon-lit service station and Marie nearly got lost in the endless corridors when she went to find the loo.

Eventually the roads grew smaller and the land more hilly, until they slowly crawled through the town of Priestcastle and up the track to Shoe Cottage.

"Come on, then!" their father ordered. "We'll just empty the car, then get you two off to bed. You can unpack properly in the morning."

Everyone bundled up bags and made a dash for the door, splashing through a yard that soaked their shoes. František found the light and switched it on. A bare light bulb revealed a tiny living-room with a poky kitchen to one side. There was one threadbare sofa and an armchair with arms worn down to the wood – no carpet, only a cold stone floor, and broken glass on the window ledge where one of the small panes of glass had fallen in. The ashes of a long-dead fire lay damp in the empty fireplace.

"Fantastický!" shouted Jan sarcastically, as he looked around. He saw a door that led upstairs. "And the biggest bedroom is mine!" He bounded up, chased by his sister. "I need more space for my growing bones!" he declared. *Older brothers are a pain*, thought Marie, *and Jan proves the point!*

The bedrooms, like the downstairs, were tiny and smelt like old dishcloths. There were no heaters and no curtains to keep out the whistling draft. As Jan and Marie bounced on the creaky beds, František was foaming downstairs.

"The agency said this was a quaint, three-bedroom cottage with central heating in the middle of the picturesque countryside!" he stormed, pulling open cupboards to reveal mouldy walls. 'Quaint' obviously had more than one meaning.

"*Ano! Ano!* Yes! Yes!" sighed Mrs Kleček as she

stepped forward to hug her husband. It was two-thirty in the morning and in a few hours it would be Franz's first staff day at Priestcastle Secondary School. He had been so proud when he was shortlisted for an interview in Prague, and then when he found he had been accepted, due to his excellent English. He wanted to give his family the experience of a lifetime, and what had they got so far? Shoe Cottage! He shook his head and ducked outside to splash across the yard to the car.

While their night things were unpacked, the children wolfed down the last of the salami, then they brushed their teeth in the damp, lime-green bathroom and leapt under thin sheets.

Their mother and father ducked into each tiny room to say goodnight. *"Dobrou noc! Spi dobře, Jane!* Sleep well, *Mařenko!"* Kisses and hugs were parcelled out and lights extinguished. The rain drummed on for a while, then died down, and even the wind seemed to give up the ghost. After much clattering and shushing, creaking and soft grumbling, finally their parents were asleep in the main bedroom. Jan lay listening for a while, before silently creeping across the landing and into his sister's room to sit on her bed.

"Are you awake, Marie?" whispered Jan. "Do you remember the house we built out of branches one summer at the bottom of our garden?"

"Yes, that was more comfortable than this!" They peered out of the window. A thin moon curled like a pig's tail in the sky.

"What are we doing here, Jan? I don't like it," Marie burst out in a fierce whisper. "It's damp and cold and feels bad. That bull was a bad omen."

"That's my sister for you!" joked Jan, poking her shoulder. "You could moan for Moravia! And anyhow, this is the countryside, same as at home. Animals are always escaping. I don't call that spooky!"

"Well, escape from this, then!" Marie hissed, flinging herself silently at Jan. "Let's see you laugh at me when I give you a dead arm!" But as usual, her brother was too quick. She gave up and sank back, exhausted, staring across at Jan in the moonlight. Light hair, like their mother, and thickly built. Their grandma Babi always used to say, "Solid as a dumpling, my boy is!"

Marie took after their father. Skinny and slight as an elf with hair black as charcoal. But her pale moon of a face had the wide Slavic cheekbones of her mother.

Tomorrow, she thought, would be her first day at school over here. What would the English children be like? She would be split up from her brother, as he would be starting at the Secondary school. She closed her eyes, trying to banish the uncertain future.

13

"I'm asleep," she murmured. "Sleep well!"

Jan crept back to his room and Marie curled tighter in the cold bed. She drifted into a troubled sleep filled with the cry of rain and wind, and somewhere in the darkness a huge bull staring at her with red eyes...

New school

"Children, I would like you to welcome Marie Kleček to our class today." Mrs Evans beamed a smile warmer than the whole of Shoe cottage. But the faces that turned to look at Marie were not quite so welcoming. "Her father is the new maths teacher at the High School," Mrs Evans carried on. "I do hope you will make her feel at home. Marie has been studying English at her school in the Czech Republic, but please help her if she gets stuck."

That first morning, the top class were starting on a project about the Romans. Marie looked at the pictures and wished she too had some armour she could hide behind. What was she doing in this strange place?

Earlier, her mother had walked with her down the track and along the lane into the small town where they were quickly lost among the alleys and winding streets. But at last, following other mothers with children, they found the school.

At the gates, Marie felt six again. She wanted to cling on to her mother, but what kind of 11-year-old did that? So she insisted she would go in by herself.

After all, she would only have to translate for her mum if she came in with her. Without turning back, she walked stiffly across the playground towards the teacher on duty.

***

"My name's Ashleigh," announced a tall girl, looking sideways at Marie. It was break-time and they were both standing at the edge of the playground. The others were playing football, but Marie was too nervous to join in – and anyway, nobody had invited her.

"*Dobrý den*… I mean, good day to you!" stammered Marie, forgetting her English for a second.

"You've got a funny way of talking!" said Ashleigh. "I've never met anyone from a foreign country before."

"Forgive me, I am start to learn English!" Marie was struggling to get the words in the right order. "Yes, in my country, vee have no electric or TV. I live in cave and ride to school on pig." Marie looked very solemnly at Ashleigh. For a second, Ashleigh couldn't decide whether Marie was being serious or not. But as Marie smiled, Ashleigh burst out laughing.

"Very good! I'm impressed! They have a sense of humour in your country too!"

Marie pulled her little dictionary out of her pocket

to look up 'humour'. "Ah, yes! Hoomore! Joke!" Marie laughed. Soon, they were using a mix of words and hand gestures to find out more about each other and Ashleigh had agreed (in mime) to lend Marie some of her glitter nail varnish, when the bell went.

Something called 'Numeracy Hour' happened next, which Marie recognised as Maths. At first, she breathed a sigh of relief, thinking that numbers on the page would be easy because she would not have to translate them. However, a loud rat-a-tat-tat of questions and answers broke out around her. Marie realised with rising panic that she could only make out one word in ten. It was so fast! She'd never be able to follow it all, let alone understand, work it out, translate and then put her hand up!

Lunch was even worse. She had to sit next to a boy who ignored her during the whole meal, if 'meal' was the right word for it. It consisted of soggy chips and

something round and brown that looked as if it would bounce. No wonder some of the children looked so unhealthy, eating food like this!

At the end of school, Marie's mother was there, waiting at the school gates. Marie could see her through the window as they were all lining up to collect their coats, and the familiar face made her feel almost tearful. As Marie rushed out, she could see that a couple of other mothers were trying to chat to her mum. But as Mrs Kleček's English consisted mostly of "Yes" and "No" and "Good, good!" it was a rather one-sided conversation.

Marie felt herself being grabbed by Ashleigh and pulled towards someone else. "Can Marie come and play at our place, Mum? Please?" Ashleigh was putting on her best whining voice. Marie looked up at Ashleigh's mother. She had blond hair with dark roots, jeans that seemed too small and little stony eyes which took a short look down at Marie and then turned away. The girl stood out from the rest of children milling about, like a colour picture in a black and white newspaper – her un-Englishness was obvious.

Mrs Jillson lit up a cigarette and flicked the lighter into her pocket. "No. There's the tea to get, your Nan to pick up from the bus. Maybe another time, eh, Ashleigh!" She ruffled Ashleigh's hair and turned her back on Marie. Marie's ears burned and Ashleigh looked squashed. She shrugged her shoulders and waved goodbye.

Marie wondered why Ashleigh's mother was so unfriendly. What had she done wrong? The way she looked at Marie, as if she was no more than a piece of chewing gum stuck under a desk! It made her feel as if she wasn't supposed to be here... As her mother chatted in Czech and asked whether she had enjoyed school, Marie just nodded her head, keeping her eyes on the pavement. They were just turning to leave when Mrs Evans rushed out. She grabbed Mrs Kleček by the hand and shook it for all she was worth.

"A delight to have you with us, Mrs Kleček! If you have time, we would love you to come to our W.I. – that's the Women's Institute!" Her smile was almost Day-Glo, and though Mrs Kleček didn't understand a word, she felt the teacher's warmth and nodded away like a hen. While Marie translated, Mrs Evans explained how the women at the W.I. brought home-made food and jams to share at their meetings. At the mention of food, Mrs Kleček's ears perked up. This was her territory! She was the cook to beat all cooks and the chance to share her food with new friends was not one to be missed. Catering for large groups was her speciality, and they shook hands once more and mother and daughter turned to walk back through the town under the warm September sun. As they approached the cottage, Marie took a proper look at their new home – it was as small and grey as it had appeared on the first night, with a holly and beech hedge at the sides and a small, unkempt garden at the back. And the house was oddly shaped – as if it had squeezed itself on to the foundations and sat down. The chimney leaned over as if trying to listen to Marie's thoughts and she wondered if the building was about to fall over.

"Now, go off and explore," Mrs Kleček instructed her children when they were back inside, "and don't come back until you have had plenty of fun! Oh, and here's a shopping list. Please pick up a few things for me on your way through town." Jan had been at home all day, helping with the unpacking. The weather had brightened after last night's storm and he felt he'd earned a break. His mother gave him twenty pounds and a long list.

"Hey, thought you said 'a few' things," he laughed. Mrs Kleček smiled and shooed them off down the track.

"How was school?" asked Jan.

"Everyone jabbers like monkeys! It's such a relief to speak Czech again… and the day goes on for ever. I thought it would never stop!"

In the Czech Republic, children began school at 8 and were finished by lunch. A row of long days spread out drearily in front of them.

As they reached the lane, Jan said, "A-ha! There is your spooky bull, Marie!" The gate wobbled as they sat on it and the bull munched grass and ignored them.

"I thought it was a nightmare," Marie replied. In daylight, the bull didn't seem nearly so frightening or so big, chewing away and flicking at flies with his tail.

"You're just like Babi, always seeing signs everywhere!"

They jumped down and followed a footpath sign through the next field and towards a line of trees, until they found themselves standing at the edge of a large lake. Geese skimmed the surface, while further away were elegant swans and, on the other side, a heron rose slowly from the water like a flapping helicopter. The path was filled with blackberry bushes. Jan and Marie looked at one another, dropped their things and plucked greedily at the September-ripened fruits.

"This isn't so bad, is it?" said Jan, as they sat down with their toes dabbling in the water.

"No! Lakes and rivers, just like home! Maybe it'll all work out!" and for a while Marie forgot about the strangeness of school. "We should pick some blackberries to take back."

"Mmmm, we should…" But Jan didn't finish. Instead, they lay back in the grass and watched the dragonflies buzz about their business.

They were almost snoozing in the afternoon sun,

when a sudden rattling voice made them sit up. Along the path, shuffling with the aid of a stick was… well, what exactly was it? It was certainly the strangest sight they had ever seen. Jan thought it might be a person, but he couldn't be sure. It was round, like an apple and covered in layers of coloured rags topped with a mop of grey-black hair. What's more, it was muttering to itself.

"It's my path, and my lake, and my swans, and you took it all, yes you did, you did, you little cutpurse, con-thief, bad burgling boy!" Jan and Marie stood stock-still as it drew nearer, until a face appeared amongst the hair, wrinkled like dried apricots, but not as sweet. The voice bore down on them, picking up volume.

"And who are you, on my land, on my grass, eh? EH?" it screamed with yellow teeth, and waved the stick like a sword as it flew towards them.

This was too much. All the peace they had felt a few moments before was smashed by this howling fury. Jan and Marie scrabbled to their feet and without looking back, made a run for it. They scrambled through the fields, and were back on the lane into town.

"Who… or what was… that?" Marie panted.

"Someone who did not want us to be there!" puffed Jan, winded. "So much for exploring…"

"And fun," added Marie. "But why did we run? She was only an old woman in a grumpy mood. I've never seen you look so scared!"

"Scared! You were the rabbit, scampering away!" They went on bickering as they made their way into town to pick up the shopping. As they crossed a stile, they could see Priestcastle laid out below them. It was an ancient market town cupped in its own valley, with most of the houses centred around one long high street, dotted with shops, that wound its way uphill like a snake to the town hall, topped by the clock-tower that seemed to be forever stuck at half-past four.

They wandered to the top of the hill and found that the castle the town was named after was no more than a crumbling bit of wall hidden away at the back of a tiny green. A sign said that when the castle had fallen into ruin in the 18th century, the enterprising citizens had stolen much of the stone to build their own houses.

"An early form of recycling!" joked Jan as they sat on a huge log that had been turned into a seat and watched the higgledy-piggledy roofs slanting away down the hill. It really was a beautiful town, the late afternoon light tinged with smoke from early-lit fires.

The supermarket seemed no different from home, apart from the fact that Jan had to decipher some of the tins, and he was flustered when it came to counting out the English money. Shoppers behind them shuffled their feet with impatience, but the woman behind the checkout counter was friendly.

They were walking back up the lane with their heavy bags when they heard the roar of a car behind them, growing louder. They turned. The car was a huge black four-by-four with a bull bar on the front. It didn't slow down, but seemed to speed up as it approached them. They both leapt back into the hedge, spilling shopping everywhere as it careered past. Marie had a glimpse of a bald man hunched over the wheel and two laughing teenagers in the back.

"Ty blbče!" Jan shouted, as he choked on the dust and bent down to pick up the crushed eggs and oranges that had rolled down the lane. But this lane was a dead end. It only led to Shoe Cottage. Whoever it was, had come to visit them.

Meeting the landlord

"Sorry about that, children!" smiled Bob Thomson, their new landlord, though he did not look sorry at all. Everything about Bob was bursting out. His old, buttoned-up tweed jacket, his too-short trousers, his strained check shirt: all threatened to erupt at any moment. Even his head looked as if it had just popped out of his shirt collar. The man was done up like a parcel. Inside his fleshy face, little piggy eyes rolled round and his skin was slightly sweaty. Marie did not need second sight to know that this was not a nice man.

"I really didn't see you as I drove up the lane!" he explained, picking at his yellowing teeth with a matchstick. "Your fault for not keeping your eyes open, of course." They were standing outside Shoe Cottage in the yard. He pulled out a sheaf of papers and peered closely at them.

"And you must be Mrs... Cluckcluck."

"Kleček!" she replied, and put out her hand. Bob Thomson instantly pulled his back. "Hmm. Can't say the agency told me you was from abroad."

"Yes! Yes! *Česká Republika*. Czech Republic."

"Never heard of it." Bob Thomson grimaced. "Don't get many from foreign parts round here." He stared at the children as if they were exotic animals from a zoo. Marie could feel her ears burning again. She looked straight back at him, eye to eye, until he was the one to give in, and, coughing, dropped his gaze.

Meanwhile, at the back of the Land Rover, the two teenagers hopped out and stood around looking bored.

"Oh yes, and these here are my great nephew and niece, Ross and Kerry." He motioned them to step forward. "They're twins. Not that you'd know from looking at 'em, eh? Say hello."

" 'Lo," they both repeated sullenly.

The world is full of friendly people... Marie thought bitterly: Ashleigh's mother, the old witch who chased them from the lake, their new landlord who obviously didn't even want them to be here – and now these two peering up at them. They had the same narrow eyes, the same cunning scowls. Ross might be light-haired and Kerry's hair a darker shade of mud, but there would be never be any mistaking those identical blunt eyes. Marie pretended to look friendly. Ross and Kerry eyed Jan with distaste and completely ignored her.

"Now, I have come here today," Bob continued in an oily voice, "to see that you have settled in all right."

Mrs Kleček began to speak quickly in Czech and point her finger at Bob, who shifted back in alarm as her voice rose in pitch. Jan stepped in immediately and put his hand on his mother's arms. He felt like a politician. If he translated exactly what she said, (and Mrs Kleček was being very direct about what a tip the house was), then Mr Thomson would either just walk away or blow up. Neither would be helpful. So Jan trod carefully around his mother's complaints. He mentioned the yard that had no drainage, the draughts round the windows, the fact there were no curtains, the damp in the living-room and the broken window. But he spoke in a friendly way, as if asking Bob for advice.

"Well now, hmmm!" Mr Thomson pretended to think. "It doesn't say anything in the contract about curtains – it doesn't sound like you've read the small print." Ross and Kerry smirked. "And what do you expect from a lovely cottage in the countryside? A little bit of damp never harmed anyone. And the rent is so cheap, I'm almost payin' you! But tell you what," he went on, as if he was doing them an enormous favour,

"I'll get my man Gus in to sort those drains and the window that you broke! Can't have our foreign guests splashing through the front door, can we?" he boomed, and slapped Jan on the back. "…Anyhow, must dash! Properties to see, rents to be sorted – and tenants to… look after! Good day to you, Mrs Clickclick!" He herded Ross and Kerry into the back of the car, slammed the doors and screeched off down the lane.

Mrs Kleček let the smile fall from her face.

"What a kind man!" Jan muttered savagely. "And the window was already broken…"

But there was no point being miserable. They would just have to make do. They got on with putting away the shopping and pinning up towels against the windows until curtains could be made. Soon the fire was lit and the aroma of dumplings filled the house. This smelt more like it! Jan and Marie were just packing cardboard under one of the table legs to stop it wobbling, when their father arrived home, looking tired but excited.

"This is wonderful! The staff have been most friendly and I have spent an excellent day with my fellow maths teachers learning about the school. Yes, I think I shall enjoy meeting the young people tomorrow!" Jan and Marie exchanged silent looks and wondered if their father knew what he was letting himself in for.

The fire crackled in the grate, and the rickety table was filled with plates of dumplings and pork in a cream and caraway seed sauce. They closed their eyes for their father to say grace. And for a second, Marie was back home with all that was familiar. She opened her eyes. Maybe home was what you took with you, halfway across the world. Maybe home was her family – and in this flickering flame-light, the cottage almost seemed cosy.

***

"Jan, Jan the Cheque-book Man!" It hadn't taken long for Ross and Kerry to find Jan on his first morning at school. "Do all you Czechs bounce then, eh? Bouncing Czechs! Shall we drop you down the stairs to find out?"

Ross's humour was about as grown-up as he was. In the corridor, between lessons, the stupid chant had followed Jan as he was looking for his next class. The whole morning had been so different, so impersonal. Although the teachers were welcoming, he had been left alone to find his way about, and the school seemed as big as a city. He wished he had a map.

"Lost your way, then?" said Kerry, chewing gum. There seemed to be a competition in the school to wear your school tie as short as possible, and both twins had little fat stubs peeking out from their undone collars. Ross was wearing a hair-cropped-so-short-it's-almost-not-there look, perhaps hoping to be as bald as his great-uncle one day.

"Don't say much, do you?" said Ross.

"What would you like me to say?" answered Jan.

"Ooh, he does speak quite the gentleman!" giggled Kerry.

"Just to let you know, mate," Ross leered closer as he spoke, and his breath stank of cigarettes, "we've got our eye on you!"

"And which eye is that?"

"Don't be clever!" hissed Kerry.

"But I am!" insisted Jan. "And I bet on my 'Czechbook' that you are not!"

They looked at each other, and Jan wished he'd kept his mouth shut. It wasn't a good idea to make enemies.

At that moment a teacher swept past, reminding them that the bell had gone.

"Later!" threatened Ross, and they both stepped back into the whirlpool of pupils. Jan kept his head down for the rest of the day. With such a large school, it was easy to lose himself in the crowd. Lunch and lessons sped by and no one took the blindest bit of notice of him, apart from during Maths, when his dad winked at him as he walked in and took a seat. If this had been home, he would have been dead embarrassed to have his dad teaching him. But now Jan was grateful for the familiar face, the known voice.

After school, there was an impromptu football match on the pitch by the sports centre. Jan looked on longingly from the side.

One of the lads, noticing Jan, shouted out, "Come on mate, we're one short."

Jan wasn't certain what 'mate' meant, but it sounded friendly enough. He pulled off his jumper and within a few minutes was showing off his footwork. The language of football did not need any translation and when Jan scored a goal, the boys clapped him on the back.

"Czech this guy out!" laughed one of his team. Jan groaned, pleased that he at least understood the awful pun, and for the next half-hour all worries were kicked away on to the sidelines.

Lady of the woods

Two weeks passed, and Shoe cottage was starting to feel more like a home. While Jan and Marie's father was teaching, their mother had been busy cleaning, sponging down walls, getting rid of cobwebs and making up curtains. Bob Thomson's handyman had repaired the broken window, but the yard still filled with water every time it rained.

Marie had settled in at school. Sometimes she found it hard to keep up in lessons. The other children spoke English so fast that all the words seemed to bump into each other. And she missed Jan. But now she had Ashleigh to sit next to at lunch.

"What's an asylum-seeker?" Ashleigh asked, as she toyed with her chips in the school hall, one rainy afternoon, "cos that's what my mum says you are."

"*Já nerozumím…* I do not understand," Marie started angrily, though she knew it was meant as an insult. "Ven vee came England, the lady who stamped passports said same."

Every time Ashleigh had asked Marie to play, her mother had come up with some sort of excuse.

"I don't think my mum likes you!" sighed Ashleigh. "But I don't care what she thinks!" she finished defiantly. Marie smiled.

"Anyhow, the other kids round here give *me* a hard time too. Because I'm tall and skinny, they call me 'Ash tree' or 'Ashtray', 'cos my Mum smokes and the smell gets into my clothes."

Marie tried to suppress a giggle – "You English have vay vith vords!" – but as Ashleigh glared at her, Marie stopped herself. "But yes, this is not so nice!"

"You don't like the letter *w*, do you?"

"Ve have not this sound in Czech. My mouth finds it…" – and Marie struggled to say what she meant – "does not like it!"

"Well, I can understand you, so that's all right. Listen, my mum's going to be out late tomorrow. She'll let me go home from school by myself and so she won't know what I'm up to. How about we go down to the river and hang out?"

The bell went and lessons began again. But now Marie had something to look forward to. After school, the rain settled in and the sky was the colour of what had pretended to be vegetables at lunch. Jan walked from his school to pick up Marie and by the time he got there, the primary school gates were deserted.

"No football today?"

"Cancelled due to this lovely English rain…"

They headed up the hill, wrapping their coats around them. After a hundred yards, Marie noticed two things: one, the streets were totally empty, and two, behind the echoing slip-slap of their feet was an echo. Overhead, the clouds seemed to grow blacker. Marie turned round, but shop doors stayed firmly shut and the alleyways were filled with shadows.

But the echo was not just her imagination. It seemed they were not alone. Suddenly a chant broke out behind them.

"Marie, Marie, quite contrary," mingled in with, "Jan, Jan, the Cheque-book Man!"

Jan looked back. "Oh great!" But it wasn't great at all. School was miserable enough, but now they were being followed home. Ross and Kerry with a couple of their hangers-on were stampeding towards them.

"Come on, Marie! Remember how you used to fly through the Moravian Woods to get home!" Marie nodded her head, as the gang gained on them.

"Get them!" shouted Ross. Jan and Marie smiled, clicked their fingers together and raced away. They had often visited their cousins in Prague and knew their way through the maze of covered arcades and walkways there like the back of their hands. It was said that if anyone was in trouble, the cousins could cross the whole city without ever going outside. Priestcastle appeared to be a similar jumble of alleys, lanes and narrow, covered passageways between buildings that locals called 'shuts'. Now they dived headlong into the maze, veering left and right and vanishing down apparent dead ends like cross-country runners.

"Where've they gone?" cried Kerry, as she came to a halt with the others, out of breath. She pulled a bit of gum from her mouth and twirled it round her fingers in frustration.

Ross had turned a shade of beetroot. "Next time, they won't be so lucky!"

But luck was with the brother and sister. They came to the end of a cul-de-sac where the houses stopped. They leapt over a stile and within seconds were in the woods. Crashing through the dark, wet woods, they disturbed a couple of roe deer. There was a flash of rusty-coloured fur and the deer melted away.

"Well done, Marenka, my black-haired raven!" panted Jan. They had reached the edge of the woods and were walking along an unfamiliar path that led to a crumbling stone barn.

"I think this leads round to the hill above our cottage. Who were those horrible people?"

"Didn't you recognise them? Ross and Kerry and their gang!" spat Jan. "I managed to avoid them at school…"

"But why do they pick on us? We've done nothing to them." Then Marie thought of the Roma girl in her

class at home and how some of the children had picked on her or refused to sit next to her, just because she was Roma and looked different. *Why do some people think these things matter?* she thought. It was so confusing.

Marie creased her black eyebrows together. "If English children came to Valašský Klobouky Basic School, I would want them to feel welcome, wouldn't you? Why don't Ross and Kerry and their friends feel like that?"

Jan shrugged his shoulders. "What can we do? Everyone thinks differently... and look at the state of you!" They were both soaked through to the skin and the rain was beating down steadily now. They hurried quickly down one side of the barn ahead, drawing level with a corrugated iron shed.

Jan pulled open the rickety door and they ran inside.

"Thought I'd see you again! Yes I did. On my land. Oh yes, indeed," rasped a voice. It was the rag woman, standing quite still, staring at them with a gleam in her eye. Jan and Marie backed towards the door.

"Sorry... many apologising... we did not mean..." It was no shed, no ordinary shelter from the rain, but something much stranger. And the old woman was advancing towards them with what looked like a sharp, forked spear in her hand, glinting horribly in the candlelight.

"We… beg… your pardon!" stuttered Jan.

"Beg, eh? You do, do you?" The woman stepped closer.

Jan opened his mouth to say something else. He was horrified to hear a scream – and then even more horrified that it was his scream, not his sister's. To make matters worse, Marie was looking at him and laughing! He blinked. The spear which had been just about to stab him now had – a crumpet on the end of it!

"Soaked! The pair of you!" exclaimed the woman. "Coats off, over the fire. Crumpets and tea to warm you up." And with that, she turned away to a blackened kettle, balanced it on top of the wood-burning stove, opened the door of the fire, and then turned back to Marie, shoving the speared crumpet towards her.

Marie took the spear and almost felt like bowing.

"I am Marie. This Jan!" she said, pointing to her brother.

"And I am Lady Beddoes. Welcome to my house!" And the rag woman did indeed speak like a lady. For a second, Marie imagined that they were taking tea in some fine English mansion, with tiny bone-china tea cups. But the crumpets dripping with butter and home-made blackberry jam and the hot sweet tea were better than any dream. Their coats steamed on the fire guard and while the rain dripped down the cracked windows, Jan and Marie peered around. What first appeared as a mess, on second inspection seemed to be a tiny, but orderly home. Shelves for plates and food stood in the corner near the fire, there was a bed on the opposite side, and a sofa pushed up close to the warmth.  Unlike Shoe Cottage, this little place felt homely.

"Shoe Cottage, eh?" said Lady Beddoes, as if reading Marie's mind. "One of Thomson's places. Hah!" She stabbed the fire with a poker as if it was the man himself. "I'm not mad, you know. The other children, they call me Barmy Beddoes, of course. Specially those brattish young relatives of his. But if I see 'em, I have a good go!" And Marie suddenly realised that when the old lady had seen them by the lake, she must have mistaken them for Ross and Kerry.

"Watch out for Bob," she went on. "If there's any apple with a worm in it, it's him, the thieving rat-bag!"

"Er, excuse me!" interrupted Jan suddenly, "I think our parents shall now be missing us."

"Course they will!" she exclaimed. "Nice to be loved. Lucky, the pair of you. Unlike me." Now she was all-a-bustle, snatching up coats and pushing the children into them, gathering plates and peering out of the window. "Storm had enough. Late afternoon, the rain just gives up and goes wherever rain goes. You go too." She began to push them out of the door. "But come back. Got a tale to tell you. About a bull. Eh, Marie?"

Marie felt a shiver go down the back of her spine. What did this strange woman know about a bull? It was as if she was reading her mind. But before Marie could say anything, the door was slammed in their faces.

The sun had come out, and by the time the children got home, their clothes were dry. There seemed no point in telling their parents about the mad woman.

The trouble with treasure

Deanna giggled. "She's mad as a hatter, that Kylie." And four other heads nodded knowingly. Mrs Evans hadn't yet arrived and as the class waited, a group of girls gathered round one of the tables.

"She came in the other day with her school sweatshirt on the wrong way round!" exclaimed Cassie. "She's round the bend, she is!" The whole table fell about laughing. *Sniping seems to be what they all do*, Marie thought, watching. She didn't have to understand what they were saying to make out the underlying meaning.

At that moment Kylie walked in. Five faces fell silent, turning towards her, and Kylie went red.

"Talk of the devil!" hissed Cassie, who was always beautifully dressed. Kylie tried to ignore them and walked to her table. Marie wondered what a *hatter* was. And *round the bend*. Did this mean that Kylie could see round corners? She pitied the poor girl, who was just a bit absent-minded, but likeable enough.

"And what are you staring at?" Cassie now turned on Marie and Marie was about to say something, when

Mrs Evans rushed in. Folders were handed out and spelling practice began. Unfriendly faces were hard enough, but Marie really struggled to spell these difficult English words. Nothing seemed logical or was spelt as it sounded. Today they were looking at *rough*, *cough* and *bough*. It was infuriating, and Marie felt her neck grow hot with the effort of pronouncing them, let alone remembering how to write them.

Playtime after lunch was the same as usual. Marie watched the group of girls who always made a point of ignoring her. She was still puzzled. It was obvious that some of them were curious about her but it seemed that roost-ruling Cassie had decided Marie was not to be mixed with. But Ashleigh wasn't bothered by these unspoken rules.

"I could see you were finding it hard there!" she said, as they lounged against a wall.

"Yes, this is not easy. Writing your vords is very difficult, but worse is ven all you speak fast!"

"I've never thought about it before. We just take it for granted." Ashleigh twirled a strand of her hair round her finger. "Words and that… Anyhow, are you up for it this afternoon?"

"Up vere?" asked Marie, totally confused.

"Oh, sorry. Yeah, right. The river…"

"Oh yes. That sounds good." Marie smiled for the first time that day.

Jan came to meet Marie after school and Ashleigh led them out of town and down the road through the valley. It was a glorious late September afternoon. They crossed a bridge over the river and turned into a small road that petered out into a footpath. Sheep protested as they walked down through a hilly field, trying to avoid the thistles. Finally they rounded a corner and there was the river curving in a lazy loop.

"The perfect spot!" Jan shouted, running the rest of the way downhill. They climbed between two strands of barbed wire and found themselves on a little pebble beach.

"My dad used to take me fishing here before he left." Ashleigh fell silent and Marie realised that she had never seen Ashleigh's father. Now she knew why.

But the sun was out and Ashleigh dared them to go in first. They peeled off socks and trainers, rolled up trousers and Marie and Jan stepped in carefully.

Freezing!

"Look!" said Marie. Baby trout were resting in the shallows, darting away each time she threw in a pebble. Suddenly, her feet slid apart on the slime of stones and she stumbled forwards.

"*Pomoc!* Help!" she screamed, grabbing at her brother's hand so that he too landed on his knees. The shock of the cold knocked their breath out in a high squeak. Ashleigh giggled as they scrambled up,

45

dripping, and together they paddled towards a high chalk bank on the other side. There they sat, skimming stones downstream. Their problems slowly slipped away and homesickness drifted off with the current.

Their trousers were still damp as they walked back along the path to town. At the clock-tower, Jan and Marie said their goodbyes to Ashleigh and headed up the hill to Shoe Cottage.

"Where have you been?" demanded Mrs Kleček shrilly. But when they told her about the river, she couldn't be annoyed. She had spent all day working on a new vegetable patch, digging, then planting a winter crop. There was still some spadework left and she was hoping for volunteers.

"But Mum, we've been slaving all day in our strange country schools, then suffering the bone-chilling rivers of Shropshire!" protested Jan.

"How about braised duck with blackcurrants?" enquired Mrs Kleček. Appealing to the goodness of children's hearts never worked, but bribery was a tried and trusted method. Two hands shot up and instructions, spades and forks were issued.

The garden was still a tangle of weeds, but their mother had made some headway. In the far corner, she had set up a small wire and wood chicken-run, and four Rhode Island Reds (the best egg-layers, according to the lady who had come to drop them off) were scratching and clucking away. She had dug a central rectangle and divided it into four. Jan and Marie set to, clearing a mass of ground elder. The sun was lower now, and somewhere from far off came the autumnal scent of burning leaves. This was soon joined by a delicious smell of cooking, floating out from the kitchen window.

It was clear that Bob Thomson, or his previous tenants, had really not looked after Shoe cottage, because the children soon discovered that the ground was full of rubbish. However, after pulling out yet more broken glass, Jan gasped excitedly as his spade hit the edge of something metallic.

"Treasure!" he exclaimed, peering down and scrabbling with his fingers at a submerged metal box. "We're going to be rich!"

Marie rushed over to see and immediately joined in, helping to dig round the edges. Together, they lifted up the rectangular shape with anticipation.

"Yes! An old rusty fan-heater! Must be worth millions of koruna!" But as she doubled over with helpless giggling, her eye caught a glint in the turned soil. She bent down.

"Jan! Come here!" In her hand, almost untouched by the mud, and shining as if straight out of a jeweller's shop, was a gold bracelet.

"Look, Marie!" Jan rubbed the earth from the

inside of the band, and they could just make out an inscription. It was engraved in a flowery style. Jan studied the words. "To... my dar... ling Isa... bella... with love... R."

This was a discovery! Marie grabbed it off her brother and they chased each other into the house, with Marie holding the bracelet out in front of her.

"Hey, Mum!" Marie shouted in English, forgetting for a second that her mother wouldn't understand. "We find this, ah, bracelet digging in garden and here some writing and... "

But before she could stop herself or her words, she ran headlong into Bob Thomson.

"And," he glowered, "what you dig up in my garden belongs to me!" He thrust out his brick of a hand and stood there, breathing in snorts. His face flashed so fiercely red that Marie wondered if she could light a fire from it.

"But we found it!" Jan complained, jutting his chin forwards. In the dark kitchen Bob seemed to grow larger, sucking all the air out of the room. He fingered and caressed the bracelet he had snatched from Marie, closing his eyes briefly before his gaze snapped back to the children.

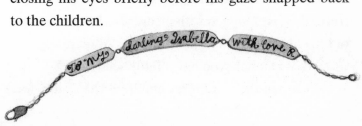

"That writing… did you read what it said? Did you?" he demanded, towering over them.

Marie thought quickly and realised that something odd was happening. "No. Is too – how you say – curly to read! We vanted show it to father to make English. But perhaps you tell us what it says?"

"On my property, what's found is for my eyes, and not for the prying of the likes of you." Bob thrust the bracelet into his pocket. Marie stared up at him as he stood with fingers bunched and shoulders heaving. She felt as though she were about to be swallowed by a huge, hungry mouth.

But Mrs Kleček had had enough. She stepped between her children and Bob Thomson and pointed at the door.

With that, Bob seemed to lose some of his puff. "I just knew you lot would be trouble," he muttered, and swivelled round and stomped out, slamming the door behind him.

***

The duck was tender and the sauce tasted of summer fruits. František sighed with pleasure as he used a piece of bread to mop up his plate.

"What manners you have, Táto!" said Jan.

"I learned them from my children!" he said before

changing the subject. "It's strange about that bracelet. Still, I guess it is his right, as he owns this house. The law would be on his side. It's a pity really, as I would like to have studied it more closely."

That's the problem with grown-ups, thought Marie. *They're too logical.*

"But Táto!"

"The subject is closed," he announced. "We may not like Mr Thomson's manners, but we must do our best to get on with people! Now, my delicious Mrs Kleček, sit yourself down while our stubborn children wash up and make us some lemon tea!"

Marie and Jan tried to make as much fuss as possible, but it was a no-win situation. While Marie was drying the dishes, she mused aloud. "Who is Isabella? And R?"

"R must be short for something, and as Isabella is a woman's name, I would say that R is, or was a man," deduced Jan. "I wonder how old that bracelet was. Pity we didn't get a closer look..."

"Well, you've finally proved you have a brain hiding somewhere deep inside your head!" said Marie.

And that night, they both went to sleep wondering why an antique bracelet should so upset an old man like Bob Thomson.

A ghostly legend

September sped by, taking with it the golden treasure of the sun. The rains had arrived, leaving the yard outside Shoe Cottage a lake and turning every road into a stream and every puddle into a pond. Marie was surprised by the number of comments about the weather. As far as she could see, the British seemed to love making gloomy remarks such as, "Another miserable one, eh?" or the more obvious "Looks like rain!" But there was truth in them, for the endless greyness and early morning fogs that refused to lift did not help matters. Jan and Marie had perfected the art of huddling in warm clothes and leaping from alley to doorway to avoid the ever-present drizzle.

***

Jan began to see school as a set of tactical avoidance manoeuvres. He knew that Ross and Kerry and their gang were out to get him. He had worked out that the toilets weren't a safe place and got away with using the disabled loo near the front entrance, where no one could wait for him. Breaks and lunch he spent in the library, and getting out at the end of school was a matter of careful timing.

But Ross and Kerry didn't give up so easily. The between-lessons scrum of pupils was perfect for tripping over, rib-punching and general jeering. Jan felt frustrated. Lessons were becoming enjoyable and at last it looked like he was going to be in the school football team. But what had he done to deserve that pair of thugs?

Everyone in class was holding their nose as the English teacher, Mrs Snead walked in.

"What is that smell?" she demanded, and walked towards the rubbish bin, lifting up a book bag to seek the source of it. "Whose bag is this?" She held it up and Jan recognised it.

"That belongs to... Mine, Mrs Snead. I thought it was under table," he answered truthfully.

From the bag, she pulled a kipper that had seen far better days.

"And is it a particularly Czech custom to eat rotten fish, Jan Kleček?"

The class laughed and Jan looked round embarrassed. "It… it was not me, Miss!"

"Something a bit fishy about all this!" said Mrs Snead, who was fond of dreadful jokes. The rest of the class groaned as she sent Jan to dispose of the fish in the wheelie bin outside. It was obvious who had put it there. As Jan walked out he spotted Doug, more commonly known as Doug the Thug, smirking at him. Doug hung about with Ross and Kerry.

"A rotten little present for you!" Doug hissed, swinging back on his chair legs as Jan walked past. Jan was pretty quick with his feet at football and now he decided to put his skills to good use.

He managed to catch the back legs of Doug's chair, hook them towards him with one foot and send the boy sprawling across the floor. The rest of the class cheered.

"That's quite enough," Mrs Snead cut in. "Now, open your books. And you," she pointed at Doug, "get up and stop messing around." Doug's eyes flashed sullenly, but he said nothing. He wasn't used to anyone standing up to him. *Ross and Kerry will know what to do*, he thought. *That Czech prat had better watch out.*

***

"I had to do something!" Jan growled as he and Marie walked home. The rain had died away leaving the streets shining like silver.

Marie smiled at the thought of the kipper in Jan's bag. "Of course you did!" she said, not really concentrating on what he was saying. "I bumped into Lady Beddoes yesterday and she invited us over for blackberry pie. I told Mum we might be a bit late."

"Well, at least someone likes us, even if she is mad!"

"As a hatter!" laughed Marie,

"What?"

"Oh, never mind, just another part of this funny country..." and they turned up through the fields towards Lady Beddoes' wilderness shed.

The chimney was puffing away like a train and the corrugated shed was dripping in the afternoon sun. As they approached, the door opened and Lady Beddoes beckoned them in.

"Come on in, then. No dawdling. I didn't invite the wind as well. Hup! Hup!" she commanded, and soon they were comfortably settled on the old sofa with hot cups of tea shoved into their hands.

"Picked these yesterday. Dark fruits. Sweet as summer!" sighed Lady Beddoes, as she handed out two huge portions. "Perfect for pies!" Jan and Marie made appreciative noises. The fire flickered in the stove and they breathed in the rare feeling of welcoming.

"Time for a tale, I think!" Lady Beddoes said, as Jan and Marie licked the last sugary crumbs from their lips.

Jan rolled his eyes in mock boredom and Lady Beddoes snapped at him, "Too old for all that stuff, eh? Eat my pie, and yet won't listen to Barmy Beddoes tell you all about the Roaring Bull of Bagbury?" At the mention of a bull, Marie felt prickles on the back of her hand and Jan's heart speeded up.

"Yes, please!" said Jan quickly. "That we would very much like."

The brief patch of blue sky vanished and the sun had given up the ghost outside, as Lady Beddoes began.

"In the long ago days of old, there was a landlord as bad as the wasp in an apple," – and here she looked at Marie and nodded her head. Lady Beddoes carried on, "He would forever be charging the highest rents and letting his properties go to rack and ruin, until the cold winters finally ruined him."

Both sister and brother thought of Shoe Cottage and wondered if the present landlord was somehow related...

"His body was broken and he died. Heaven would not take him, nor Hell neither, so his spirit walked the hills and slowly assumed the shape of a bull. Every night he roared up and down the green lanes and the sound was enough to destroy all decent and law-abiding sleep!"

At that moment, a gust of wind rattled the corrugated iron. Marie jumped up in fright.

"It's not the weather you should be afraid of, my dear girl!" sighed Lady Beddoes. "As I was saying... All the people of Bagbury and Hyssington were terrified and the parson was summoned. He knew about these things and concluded that the only solution was to 'read' the ghost down. So, early one evening, many men and women gathered together in a great circle around the ghostly bull and began to read the Bible to him. At length they herded the ghost-beast into the church at Hyssington, and there he began to shrink under the power of the Holy Word."

She paused for a moment, as if gathering her own words.

"But the light of day began to fall," Lady Beddoes continued, "and without light, the reading stopped. The ghost started to grow again until he filled all Hyssington church, squeezing and expanding until finally, with his great size, he cracked the walls. Visit the church with your parents, dear children, and you will still see the cracks."

Jan knew of the church because Will, his football friend, lived in the house beside it, though he had never mentioned the story. And something about Lady B's voice was different too, as if the tale were telling her, speaking through her to them.

"By the greatest fortune, a traveller, a stranger, a wanderer from far lands came by with a lantern. It is always the outsider who sheds light on the situation… and by the light of his flickering lamp, the villagers continued reading the ghost down until it was the size of a child's foot, small enough to be trapped inside an old shoe, with the laces tightly tied. The people danced with joy as the stone lintel step at the church door was lifted and the shoe buried underneath. The bull was gone for ever! Forever trapped! Though it is said, if ever the Roaring Bull of Bagbury is set free, then this land will be laid to waste!"

Lady Beddoes clapped her hands as if ending a spell, shaking the children out of their dreaminess. Outside, dusk was falling and the grey sky was slowly dissolving into night.

"It's all in the shoe!" muttered Lady Beddoes.

"What do you mean?" asked Marie, remembering the bull running down the lane towards them.

"What was I saying, dears?" she went on. "Oh yes, time to shoo. Back to the real world of thieves, land snatchers and him – yes, – him!" Their welcome, like the fire in the stove, had almost gone out. Coats were fetched and the children quickly pushed out into the cold to wander back through the dark woods.

Marie started, as an owl called above them.

"Look at you, little sis! Jumping at every sound!"

teased Jan. "Your imagination is too big for your body!"

Marie frowned. "But what if it was more than a tale? And what was all that about a shoe?"

"I think our wild woman of the woods spends too much time by herself!" answered Jan. But underneath his bravado, the story disturbed him. They hurried back through the dripping trees to Shoe Cottage – where an unpleasant surprise awaited them.

Mirror, mirror on the wall

As they came up the lane, they heard shouting. Jan and Marie ran the last hundred yards and were about to run in, when they realised it was their parents. They were arguing.

"But they never argue!" whispered Marie.

"And he came charging in here, demanding rent!" wailed their mother

"How dare he!" shouted František.

"And I thought you had paid it. And he was shouting at me until I was nearly in tears and you should have given him the money and…"

"Wait, Eva. Wait! I have had problems setting up a bank account. It's difficult for foreigners to do this. The bank staff were very helpful, but there are many rules about this sort of thing. I told the agency and they understood."

"Understood? Understood!" she screamed. "I do not understand this country. I hate it. Why are you always being so reasonable, and leaving me at home to deal with overgrown bullies? I'll… I'll…" Eva started sobbing and the argument died down.

Jan and Marie were shocked. They waited outside for five more minutes and then opened the front door. Their father and mother were hugging each other and Eva wiped her eyes as she saw them both come in.

"All you all right, Maminečko?" asked Marie. There were many words for "mum" in Czech and Marie used the one that was the most sweet and caring.

"Yes, my Maruško. Nothing to worry you about!" She stroked Marie's hair. "And how was school today?" And since both parents said nothing about their argument, Jan said nothing about the rotten kipper and the rotten time he was having at school. After all, Dad was enthusiastic about the school, and anyway, the practice of not telling tales was as common in the Czech Republic as it was here in their new home.

***

"Home, sweet home! All mine!" sighed Bob Thomson, as he looked in the full-length mirror. The mirror reflected back the grandeur of Bagbury Hall. High ceilings, with doors fit for giants and so many rooms he didn't know what to do with them. Half of them lay empty, the furniture covered in drapes, as if the house had gone to sleep. Bob didn't have many friends, so he often talked to himself. Now he was struggling with the top button of his shirt. It seemed he could not stop himself expanding.

"After all," he mused, "a man has to eat, and if there's no-one to share it with, it's all the more for him." The button finally surrendered to his stubby fingers, he pulled his tie tight and squeezed his tweed jacket over his bulk. It was then that he remembered the bracelet.

"Curse and cross them all!" he muttered, as he pulled the golden bracelet out of his jacket pocket. "Has history come back to haunt me?" He poked his finger at the mirror, which said nothing. Then his eye caught the reflection of a portrait. He turned round to look up at the imposing figure of a sad-looking old man with a wrinkled sack of a face almost hidden between huge, mutton-chop sideburns. The man was dressed in stiff, formal Victorian clothes, posed with a graceful, grey lurcher dog.

"And what do you want, Vinstead? No point following me round with your eyes! You went to the dogs in the end, eh, not-so-great-grandfather! And what's the point about the shoe, eh?" The man in the portrait was wearing only one, silver-buckled shoe. "Footloose and fancy free?"

The door to his dressing-room opened. "Did you want something, Mr Thomson? I thought I heard voices…" enquired the housekeeper, Mrs Hooper.

"No, woman, just keeping myself company."

No wife to nag him, no children trying to squeeze him for money. It was all his until the day he died. Bob dismissed his sister-in-law with a flick of his hand and she retreated nervously. He was definitely getting worse. It was a clever cruelty of his, employing his widowed sister-in-law, Enid to keep house and cook. And how she managed to scrape together the rent each month from the tiny pittance he paid, nobody knew. Appealing to the bonds of family meant nothing to Bob Thomson. Even worse for Enid, he had taken a shine to her two grandchildren, Ross and Kerry.

"It'll all be yours, one day, boy," he loved saying to Ross. Perhaps he was genuinely fond of his great nephew and niece. But he also liked reminding everyone that it was he who held the purse strings. The Bagbury Estate was a strange beast in legal terms. It was common knowledge that it always went to the oldest surviving male relative, and only through the bloodline. Always had. Always would. So Mrs Hooper's son-in-law didn't count, and she and her daughter would end up the losers. The old widow tidied away the dinner. There was nothing fair in this world.

Bob left by the main doors and looked round at the house and grounds. *Very grand indeed. If only Father could see me now.* The tall pillars flanked the front door and the whole gloomy stone building, with its rows of

dark windows, seemed to lean over him. And the privacy of a house hidden in thick jungle suited his temperament well. He roared off down the drive.

At the Five Bells, Bob shouldered his way in front of two men waiting to be served. They knew better than to cross one of the main employers and largest land-owners in the area.

"A pint of your Castle Best!" A few drinks later, and he was in full flow. "I mean, why couldn't they get someone from round 'ere to teach 'em a bit of maths?" he declaimed to anyone who would listen. "He can't even speak the lingo proper!"

"Actually," muttered Ben Wall, one of the teachers at the college, "he speaks it better than you."

"What was that, Ben Wall? You disagreein' with me?"

Ben Wall shrank under his stare. "Nothing, Mr Thomson."

"Yeah. Nothing!" Bob carried on. "They're just nothings. And always complaining about the cottage. They had the nerve to say that my Derek escaped from his field and attacked their car!"

As everyone knew Derek to be the most ill-tempered beast, like his owner, they were not surprised. But Bob was even more foul-mouthed that usual. Some change seemed to have come over him as he ranted on and on about the Klečeks. They gathered closer around him, nodding their heads, and after an evening of beer, it was easy to agree with anything. As they lurched out of the pub at closing time, a sense of mischief and malice pervaded the air.

Event in the church

"Four flat tyres! It can't be a coincidence!" František knelt down to investigate. It was not a long walk into town, but today he had a maths training morning in Shrewsbury. The work had been hard so far this term. He was desperate to fit in and prove what a good teacher he was, and the late nights of marking were beginning to show. He had moon-like bags under his eyes and now the worry lines in his forehead furrowed even deeper.

"Evo! Evo!" he shouted. Every tyre had deep marks in it, where it had been slashed with a knife. Jan and Marie came running out with their mother. Marie felt so sorry for the poor old Škoda that she almost wanted to hug it. "I must call the school…" and he ran in to see if anyone else in the department could pick him up.

"Ježiš-Maria!" said Eva over and over again, as she fingered her rosary beads.

"Who would do this?" asked Jan.

"Ross and Kerry wouldn't dare – would they?" said Marie angrily.

"Shhhh!" said Jan and grabbed Marie. Eva was looking distractedly at the car. Luckily, she hadn't been listening. She had no idea that there were problems at school and Jan wanted to keep it that way.

Their father came back out. He had managed to get a lift and ring the local garage to take the car away. There was nothing more they could do. It was not as if the police would come finger-printing for a simple case of vandalism. František walked down into town with the children and Eva shrugged her shoulders and got on with the day.

***

"I've been learning all about bodies today," Marie said, when Jan picked her up from school later that afternoon. "We've been drawing skeletons. Did you know that there are twenty-seven bones in each ankle and foot!"

"Fascinating!" yawned Jan. "Listen, Marie, one of my football friends, Will Gee, has invited me to play on his computer. His mum's picking me up here in five minutes."

"Great!" said Marie. "Though I can't say that shooting at imaginary beasts all afternoon is my idea of fun."

"Did I say you were invited?" Jan asked, rolling his

eyes. "Can't you go home by yourself? We'll stop by the phonebox and tell Mum when to expect you."

Marie was shocked. "But we do everything together," she protested. "And what if Kerry sees me? And…" She hated herself for behaving like this. Part of her knew it was good that Jan was finally making friends, but another part of her was jealous. Yes, she had Ashleigh as a friend. But Mrs Jillson wouldn't let Ashleigh come over to play and the sky would turn to blueberry pie before she was invited to Ashleigh's house. So she was dependent on her brother. Whatever he did, she wanted to do too. She sensed change and she didn't like it.

Jan couldn't think of a good response. It was really uncool to have your little sister hanging round. What would Will think?

"Well… um…" Jan was trying to think of a solution when Mrs Gee pulled up. She wound down the window.

"You must be Jan's sister! Are you coming back for tea?" she smiled. Jan went red with embarrassment. He could see Will scowling in the back.

"Thank you, Mrs Gee, that is most… kind." And Marie hopped in the back with the boys, who managed to ignore her all the way back to Hyssington. The moment they arrived, the two boys piled out and vanished into Will's room.

"Boys!" said Mrs Gee, with a conspiratorial air. After she had plied Marie with a tasty home-made scone, passed her the phone to ring her mum, and asked about Marie's family, Mrs Gee mentioned the church.

"Maybe you should explore. There's a great story attached to our church next door."

Marie shivered suddenly, even though the Rayburn stove was filling the kitchen with a warm glow. "You mean the Bagbury Bull! … Lady Beddoes – "

"Oh, you've met her? Not so bad or mad really. Old as the hills she is, though I've never quite understood why she calls herself 'Lady'. Maybe she was grand once, who knows?" Mrs Gee began to unpack her shopping. "Anyway, the church is on the left. You can see it over the hedge. It's worth a look."

Marie slipped out and turned through the church gate. As she turned round, she could see the hills spread out before her, a feast of field and forest with autumn's gold now turning ragged at the edges. Priestcastle was hidden in a dip behind a hill.

It was when she walked into the shadowy church that Marie began to feel uneasy. She immediately spotted a huge crack running down the back of one of the whitewashed walls.

"Of course, old buildings shift about," she explained to the empty church.

"About, about, about!" the walls echoed back. On

70

the pulpit, a huge brass eagle leered at her, and sitting on top was a bible that must have weighed as much as a pig. She wandered round the pews and looked at some of the memorial stones. In one corner, almost covered in dust, she made out a name:

VINSTEAD BEDDOES
1850–1917
Give him rest and let him be
in blessed sleep for eternity.

And on the same plaque, but in different lettering:

RICHARD BEDDOES
youngest son of Vinstead and Mary
1894–1917
He gave his life for English soil
And now shall rest from battle's toil.

Marie was fascinated, but felt sad for a son who died in the same year as his father in a long-ago war. But it was their last names that leapt out at her: Beddoes. She sensed that Lady Beddoes had been around these hills for a very long time. Maybe they were her ancestors? Then, as Marie came back to the door, she saw another plaque bearing the words *The Roaring Bull of Bagbury.*

Underneath, in a plain, wooden frame, was the story that Lady Beddoes had told them, though some of the details were different. In this version, the Bull ended up in a boot, not a shoe, before the laces were tied tightly. Some of the language was old-fashioned. However, the person who had written this treated the story like a good fairy tale, keeping you guessing what would happen next. Marie picked up one of the leaflets that were neatly stacked under the framed story. It contained a copy of the tale and information about the writer. In the 19th century, a woman called Christina Burne had gone round the countryside collecting folklore, a bit like the Brothers Grimm. She had written down all the tales and superstitions that farmers and shepherds, widows and wheelwrights and the other local people had told her. The leaflet finished: *But as far as the Bagbury Bull is concerned, of course it was only a good ghostly tale for a winter's night.* Marie wasn't so sure about that.

"Time to be getting back," she thought. The sky was darkening outside and rain began to fall. She felt nervous about crossing the doorstone. Was there really an imprisoned spirit underneath?

Marie had just wrenched open the heavy, studded door when something jolted her sideways, and she stumbled. The floor itself seemed to shiver and through the door she saw the lights in the lane below go out. Another shifting jolt, and one of small windows high up in the church shattered, sleeting ancient stained glass down right in front of her. For a second she crouched in total shock. Then she opened her mouth and screamed as she'd never screamed before. She knew, just knew that the door-stone was about to lift up and the old Bull of Bagbury come back to life. She hesitated, then rushed wildly through the doorway, running like the wind over broken glass, past the gravestones and round to Mrs Gee's house.

She hurtled in through the door and flung herself at Mrs Gee, sobbing:

"*Bože, Bože! Já mám strach!* The Bull! The Bull! I did not do it! I did not lift doorstone, how could I? But he has to life come back and is my fault!" She stared around the kitchen and realised with mounting horror that it was filled with flickering candles. Now she understood: some door had opened on the past and soon, they would have to march out and face the beast, armed only with a bible!

"Marie! Marie! Calm yourself! There's no bull, except in a wonderful old story, and that's where he will stay. I suppose they haven't told you about our local earthquake tremors at school yet, have they?"

"*Já nerozumím…* I mean… I do not understand!" Mari looked around the room in a panic, as though bracing herself for the Bull to charge in.

74

"Earthquake, when the ground shakes a lot!" explained Mrs Gee in a soothing voice. "We had a big tremor back in the summer. It rattled all my china on the shelves, it did. They said there might be more this autumn. You see, Shropshire has a fault line deep down under the earth. We can go years without the slightest murmur, then two or three little shakes in a row. Never anything major though, only the odd broken cup. We're pretty safe, according to the scientists!" She quietly touched the wooden table behind her, to be sure.

Marie had been only half-listening. "Earth squeak? How you say? Oh, earthquake. Yes!" She wiped her eyes and came back to reality. "Yes. That is it?"

"It is, Marie, and it has an annoying habit of knocking out the electric, too."

"That's for sure!" said Will as he stormed in. "And I was trashing Jan on the fifteenth lap of Silverstone when the screen went dead!"

"Ha! Maybe you can drive imaginary car faster than me but watch out for me on pitch!" countered Jan. "What is the matter, Marenka? Have you seen a ghost?"

Marie burst out crying again.

"I think," said Mrs Gee, heading off any trouble, "that it's time I got you two back home." Marie gave her brother a look so sharp it could cut hair, and his new friend stayed silent in the car all the way back.

Their mother was waiting at the door as they climbed out. Jan quickly explained in Czech about earth tremors as Marie ran to her mother's arms.

"Thank you! Thank you!" said Mrs Kleček to Will's mother. "Tea?"

"No, no, thank you very much, Mrs Kleček! I have to be getting back to put the dinner on for Will. But another time would be lovely."

Their mother nodded and smiled as Mrs Gee turned the car and disappeared down the track.

***

Later that night after a warming meal of goulash and sauerkraut, Marie curled up in the chair nearest the fire, her thoughts running over and over what had happened earlier. Her father was busy fiddling around with the electric lights, pinning up a new cable, which meant that they had to light candles for ten minutes while he switched off the main supply. Marie shivered, remembering the candles in Mrs Gee's kitchen.

"There! Ready!" František flicked a switch that turned on an outdoor sensor light. "To show up any unwelcome visitors," he explained, on his way out to park the car with its four new tyres, right by the front door.

"I am just taking precautions, Evičko," he answered, when his wife quizzed him later. But every time a fox went past or the wind blew too hard, the bright arc light flashed on and the children jumped up and raced to the window. František shook his head and hoped that last night was just a one-off incident.

***

"If you had been at the church, you wouldn't be laughing," said Marie fiercely, as they sat in Jan's room that night. They were huddling under a blanket to keep out the cold.

"Oh, come on, Marie, you just let your imagination run away with you!"

And Marie knew it was not just that she was angry with Jan about his teasing. After all, Jan had always teased her. But she couldn't bring herself to admit that she was jealous of his new friendship. Yes, she was friends with Ashleigh, but she only got to see her at school. And all the other girls in her class were in thrall to Cassie and hardly spoke to her.

"You know, we should ask Lady Beddoes about her family and that stone on the church wall," she went on.

But Jan seemed to have lost interest. "Yeah, yeah! Look Marie, it's been a long day and I'm tired as a dog!"

"You are a dog!" she sniffed, and stomped off to her freezing room to bury herself under the blankets. She woke up only once, when the lights came on outside the house. She ran to the window, almost hopeful of seeing someone caught in the light, but it was an owl, startling in its whiteness, vanishing into the night.

A score to be settled

It might be nearly the end of October, but Marie was determined. This was the first opportunity she had had to swim in the sea.

"Come on Jan! Don't be such an old walrus!" she screamed, catching a wave and riding it to shore. It was a simple matter of lifting the boogie board just when the wave reached its peak and then letting its force carry her all the way up the beach. Jan didn't look too sure.

"But it's cold!" he whimpered, standing only ankle-deep at the edge. When one of the teachers in their father's department had offered them her holiday cottage on the Welsh coast over half-term, Jan had imagined looking at the sea, not getting in it!

"Aren't we getting too old for all this?" he complained. "We should be hanging round in the arcades and getting into trouble! At least it would be warmer!"

But Marie ran up to him, grabbed his arm and pulled him sharply forwards. *Splash!*

"Just you wait! You'll regret that!" But she had

dived away and was now laughing, treading water at a safe distance. Jan admitted defeat. It wasn't so bad after all, once he got used to the cold. Within a few minutes he was trying to steal her boogie board and they were seeing how far up the beach they could be carried.

After hot showers back at the cottage and a plate of fish and chips, their bodies were glowing from the inside out. Their father's worry lines had vanished and their mother was enjoying the well-equipped kitchen, cooking up feast after feast. Compared to Shoe Cottage, this was luxury.

"I wish we could take those waves home with us," mused Jan. "I mean, I love the rivers in Moravia, but for our first taste of the seaside, it isn't bad at all."

The days whizzed by and soon the packed Škoda was crawling back over the mountains in thick fog, into November and a sharp change of weather.

"That's odd!" exclaimed František, as the car

crawled up the lane to Shoe Cottage. The intruder light hadn't come on and the house seemed half-formed in the darkness. He left the headlights on and rummaged for the keys. He pushed open the door, shivering, for the house was colder inside than out. Not a single light was working.

"Must be a power cut!" said František, as they stumbled around with torches inside. Eva found candles and asked the children to get the fire going, while their father hunted for the electricity company's emergency number:

"Yes. Yes... are you sure? No power cut?... My account number?...Wait a minute..." He was cradling the phone round his neck and trying to read the electric bill by candle light. "Here we are... what do you mean? But that is impossible!" he spluttered. "No... We are still here and I don't know who..."

He slammed down the phone. "Somebody has rung the company, told them we were vacating the house and to cut off the electricity. They gave our name and account number – everything!" František was fuming. All the peace of the last few days disappeared like smoke up a chimney.

"They say they can put it back on tomorrow. But they didn't even say sorry!" František was pacing up and down the small living-room. "Who wants us to leave, do you think? Well, I will not!" he shouted,

"I won't be driven out!" Eva took his arm, but he gently shook her away. Instead, he snatched up the phone again.

"Mr Thomson!" he began strongly when a voice came on the end of the line. But Bob Thomson denied all knowledge of it and blamed the agency for a mix-up over one of his other rental properties.

"Ha! Well he would! That man is a liar and no gentleman!" said František, as they all huddled round the fire. Marie wished she could say something to cheer her father up.

"But Taťko, our holiday was magical!" she ventured.

"Yes! Yes, you are right, Maruško! Tomorrow is another day!" And trying to force a smile, he hugged his family close.

***

School started again after the break. The electricity was switched back on and stayed on. The car tyres remained plump. And the month of November was unusually bright. The weak, low sun rested in the bare branches of beech trees. Gangs of crows wheeled around the sky and bullied the larger but slower buzzards.

All seemed calm. Eva Kleček was busy cooking for a W. I. demonstration evening and František was still up all hours marking, but he gradually reached the top of each mountainous load. Ross and Kerry were keeping a low profile. But Jan was not one to let sleeping kippers lie! Especially if an opportunity presented itself.

Jan was preparing for an after-school football match. There were a few supporters gathering in little groups on the sidelines, in spite of the damp greyness that threatened drizzle. He spotted Ross and Kerry from the corner of his eye. They were hanging about, slightly apart from the others, and he took careful note of exactly where they were standing.

"What is it with football, that it must be played at the muddiest, coldest time of year?" Jan puffed, as he trotted on the spot to warm up.

"Well, it's called the British stiff upper lip!" answered Will cheerfully, stripping down to his shorts and not taking the blindest bit of notice of the biting wind.

"Stiffuppalip! is that something you take to warm you up?" Jan could not get over the endless odd English phrases that seemed to bear no relation to what they were describing.

"Yeah, something like that!" smiled Will. They were in with a good chance against D.H. Lawrence Secondary – though to Jan's mind, the other team all seemed to be built like tractors.

"Listen, Will!" Jan motioned to Will to come closer, "I have idea!" And as he explained, a mischievous grin flowed over Will's face.

A coin was flipped and Priestcastle took the opening kick. The twenty or so brave spectators were swathed in scarves, their eyes swivelling back and forth as the ball seemed to take on a life of its own, moving swiftly between the halves. However, the game got off to a bad start when the away team gained control. They executed a series of skilful passes, followed by a glancing header from their beefy captain. Goal! Priestcastle were down one-nil.

A couple of hangers-on joined Ross and Kerry and they grouped together on one side of the halfway line, trying to avoid the huge, muddy puddle that lay in the hollow behind them. It seemed that they had not really got the hang of football matches: that is, to support your own team! When the goal was scored, they cheered, and when Jan had the ball under his feet, they jeered.

Jan ignored them and focused on the game. As a centre forward, he was fast on his feet and could zip up the far line, ready for the long pass. But it was as if every kick he managed to place was right into the goalie's arms. But Jan had a different score to settle and his chance came just before the second half. The other captain was an expert at elbowing, kicking and

pulling shirts to get the ball, but this time the referee had spotted him and a free kick was given to the home team. The ball was inside the Priestcastle half, so the opposite defence did not expect him to go for goal, but just in case, they drew up in a line.

Jan glanced meaningfully at Will as he placed the ball on the ground, and Will ran off to take his position right at the edge of the pitch in front of Ross. Jan trotted back to take a run-up and as other team members shouted, "To me! To me!" he delivered the kick. As his foot connected, all his hate and anger was directed into the ball and the resounding crack of boot hitting leather echoed round the pitch. Jan was reknowned for his incredible aim and this held true as the ball bombed through the air towards Will. On cue, another boy in the Priestcastle team pretended to stumble against the referee. Will ducked as though to take it as a header, but didn't rise again quick enough and half a kilo of wet leather smashed into Ross's face.

"Bull's-eye!" roared Jan as the ref looked round, having missed what had just happened. Ross grabbed at his nose, feeling the rush of blood, lost his balance and fell against Kerry, who knocked back into Doug until, like dominoes, the whole gang toppled into the muddy puddle. The rest of the Priestcastle spectators could be heard loudly drawing a breath before going wild to see the universally-disliked bunch balled out.

"So here it is, Muddy Christmas, Everybody's having fun!" someone struck up, and soon everyone was joining in the song. For once, Ross was defeated and the gang, wetter but not wiser, hauled themselves up and slunk away muttering.

All this time, the D.H. Lawrence team were scratching their heads, trying to work out exactly what was going on. But the success of Jan's plotting seemed to give Priestcastle renewed strength, and in the second half Jan's corner connected with Will's foot and the score was equalised. To round off the afternoon, in the last two minutes one of their defence threw the ball back to the goalie, whose fingers suddenly fumbled and the ball trickled in. In the showers, Jan was hero of the match and felt the rare joy of being praised.

Revenge is not so sweet

For an old bag, Widow Smethwick is raring to go, thought Coral Jillson. She wouldn't normally be seen dead in a Women's Institute Meeting. But if Coral wanted the cat fed when she took Ashleigh away on holiday, she knew she had to give in to her neighbour's request. She went out of the house and slammed the door. Ashleigh could microwave something from the freezer later. *Phew* – it was cold enough out here. And what was worse, was the pace that Widow Smethwick set. Accompanying her wheeled zimmer frame was like taking a snail for a walk.

"Wonderful demonstration tonight, my dear!" she wittered on. "Wouldn't miss it for the world. A demonstration of Czech cookery! How delightful to sample the fare of different cultures!"

Coral Jillson wasn't listening to a word. She tried to nod every so often to look as if she was interested.

Light spilled on to the pavement and a hubbub of voices could be heard as they passed into the warmth of the town hall. Ashleigh's teacher, Mrs Evans came bounding over, shook her hand vigorously and ushered the Widow to a nearby seat. Mrs Jillson suddenly felt very nervous and hovered at the edge of things as the meeting got under way. A wonderful smell filled the air and as she glanced up, a plate was passed under her nose. She grabbed the small doughy ball and dipped it in the accompanying sauce. Mmmm!

She kept her eyes on the plate and grabbed a second one.

"This is fantastic! Who made these?" she asked out loud, but as she looked up, she nearly choked.

"I am glad you admire the cooking of my mother!" said Marie, with a wicked smile on her lips.

That girl! It seemed that Marie was there to help serve and translate her mother's Czech descriptions such as 'plum dumplings in butter sauce'. And suddenly, there was Mrs Kleček smiling, with her hand stretched out towards Ashleigh's mother.

Coral Jillson could hardly ignore the woman whose national cuisine she was gobbling down. She held out a limp hand.

"Nice to…" She was clearly struggling with the word 'nice'. "Nice to… meet you!" she finally managed, red in the face with the effort of being friendly. Marie sensed a wonderful opportunity. She whispered in her mother's ear. Mrs Kleček quickly grasped the situation and delivered a sentence in Czech with the word 'Ashleigh' in it.

"My mother vould love to have Ashleigh for tea this week!" Marie translated. "Vould that be OK with you?" Coral had absolutely no choice in front of all these other women, and a day was set. As Marie walked away, triumphant, Mrs Kleček squeezed her hand.

"Aren't those Czechs wonderful!" warbled Widow Smethwick, as she tottered home. "What a cook! Apparently she managed a café back at home – had to ask her sister to take it over for the year. That sweet little girl of hers was telling me all about it. Such a joy to find out about different places, don't you think, Mrs Jillson?"

By this point, Coral Jillson had given up the fight. "Yes, Mrs Smethwick!" she said, and was glad when she could finally close the front door on the dreadful evening. But the memory of those glorious dumplings hovered just at the back of her tongue.

***

"You should have seen her face!" said Marie to Jan that night, as they sat in front of the fire while their parents were drinking coffee in the kitchen.

"I think both of us have done well today!" he replied, and told her the story of goals, noses and mud. Marie's room was now so cold that František had brought her mattress down to the living-room so she could sleep in front of the fire. It made the perfect evening den and Jan had no desire to retreat upstairs.

"But that's favouritism!" complained Jan, when their parents reappeared. "My room's an ice-box too!"

"My dear Jan, when you are old enough to apply for a job, will you put down your main skill as professional complaining?" laughed Jan's father. Their mother had saved some of the dumplings for a late pudding and when the children went to bed, they dreamed of just desserts.

***

Lady Beddoes had been sleeping badly in her camp bed. Earlier that week, the local young thugs had been around again and smashed one of her windows. And their insults were never original: "You should be locked away!" "Madly-mental-fruit-and-nut-case!" and the most hurtful, "Barmy Beddoes!" were the cleverest words they could hurl. The clouds had been threatening for days and November was coming to an end in a wash-out. When the weather finally broke, the dried-up streams woke up, the rivers roared back into life and worried farmers gave thanks for the downpour.

From where Lady Beddoes was standing, she had a commanding view over the town and the surrounding fields, and her eyes, though old, were as sharp as the sparrowhawk's claws. She spotted what looked like two of the troublemakers crossing a field far below. Her nose twitched. There was a bad feeling in the air. She wanted to turn away. After all, everyone else kept themselves to themselves.

"They mind their own business and care nothing for me!" she muttered, "so why should I care for them, eh?" But instinct turned her feet forward, and she, who had lost everything, had no fear of a few unruly teenagers.

**

Jan and Marie were also caught in the downpour.

"Where do they get the phrase, 'raining cats and dogs'?" laughed Marie, as she felt the rain forcing its way down her back.

"The British are barking mad!" said Jan, trying out the joke.

"Oh no! I am going to die laughing!" replied Marie. "You should give up your school career this minute and be offered your own television series!" They were running out of town, their trainers squelching through mud and puddles. And straight ahead, blocking the lane, were Ross, Kerry, Doug and two more boys, patiently waiting.

Ross had a huge plaster bridging his nose. He looked almost comical, but Jan and Marie weren't laughing.

"One goal down! Time to even the score!" Ross shouted, and charged towards them. Jan and Marie had no choice. There was another lane on the left, with high hedges keeping out the gloomy half-light and turning the way ahead into a dark tunnel. They ran straight into it. After a few hundred yards, the lane became a dead end, with the only exit a farmyard. The gate was open and without thinking, they ran straight through. Maybe they could ask the farmer for help? But the place seemed deserted. A few penned-in cattle stood around miserably as the huge barns loomed over them.

"Perhaps we can hide!" suggested Marie, pausing for breath. Then she looked up, and saw that their way was blocked by one of the gang. They had no choice but to turn into the yard. Another gate lay open directly in front of them, and, what with the messy yard and the rain streaming into their eyes, the ground beyond the gate just looked like more mud.

Jan and Marie both tore on through. But instead of meeting solid earth, their feet... sank.

"Aighhh!... what... ?" They fell forwards and their

hands and arms sank away from them too. *"Ne, ne!"* What was happening? Now their legs had been sucked down into the brown-green sludge. They were nearly waist deep, and worse, it stank. Jan flailed his arms and managed to twist round.

"That's another fine mess we got you into!" jeered Ross, who had caught up with the others as they stood on the edge of the slurry pit and surveyed the scene.

"I always said they were a pair of stinkers!" joined in Kerry.

"Well done! Very clever!" said Jan sarcastically, trying to look as if wading waist-deep in cow-poo was the most natural thing in the world. Marie could feel tears pricking the edge of her eyes. But she would never let these ugly fools have the satisfaction of seeing her cry.

Jan had sunk beyond his armpits, until his feet finally touched the bottom. But he was stuck fast, like fish in aspic jelly.

"Help!" Marie suddenly shouted. "I can't…" Jan realised with a flash of horror that she was still sinking, and he couldn't reach her.

"You must try to swim!" he yelled, but Marie was struggling too hard to hear.

"Help us!" Jan pleaded, turning to the gang at the edge, but they were shuffling awkwardly and trying not to look at each other.

"A bit of a laugh, you said?" Doug muttered to Ross accusingly. "What we gonna do?" They had all stopped laughing, and Kerry looked nervous.

"Yeah! Well!" Ross was trying to think on his feet, and edging away from the pit, "I think we'd better... it's not that deep... they'll be fine!" and before anyone could stop him, he ran off like a rabbit. As if on signal, the others scattered.

Marie screamed, but the wind squashed her voice. She was nearly up to her shoulders and she could feel the weight of gravity sucking her down.

"The more you move about, the quicker you sink!" Jan cried, desperate to reach her. In a minute she would be under the surface. He was only a metre away from her… but he just couldn't move any closer. Marie's mind raced, working out how long she could hold her breath and how long she had left… She had never felt so frightened. She closed her eyes and began to say the prayers her mother had taught her. The cows sensed something wrong and began to shift about. Their bellows echoed round the farmyard. Marie was literally up to her neck in it. Any moment now she would vanish for ever.

She opened her eyes. In front of her hovered a broom handle. She looked up and there stood Doug at the edge, holding the other end. Marie slithered her arms up out of the slurry to grab the end and he braced his feet. There was a slurping sound and, inch by inch, Marie was slowly dragged to the edge and heaved out. She lay there in the pouring rain like some primeval creature newly hatched from the slime.

"Is she… OK?" Jan shouted.

"Yeah, think so," said Doug, as he leaned out again with the broom handle. Jan grabbed hold, but the slurry did not want to let go of its second prize so easily. Marie was still shaking uncontrollably, but she hauled herself up and staggered towards Doug, clamped her arms round his waist and helped pull. And suddenly the slurry was losing. With a final slurp, it let Jan go and he too was slumped at the edge of the pit. Marie let go of Doug and stared at him. He dropped the broom handle and tried to avoid her gaze.

"Kippers is one thing, but…" He was lost for words and suddenly Jan felt sorry for him. He had seen the way Ross treated Doug like dirt. Maybe it wasn't all so clear-cut after all.

"Thank you…"

At that moment a roar exploded from the side of the yard and a bundle of rags came speeding towards them. The roar became a scream, accompanied by a whirling stick. Doug was terrified. He took one look at the approaching figure, turned and scurried into the dusk.

Lady Beddoes did a good imitation of a cackle. "Haven't felt so young in years! Got one of them as they came out the yard. 'Barmy Beddoes!' 'Banshee Beddoes!' That's what they called me. I whacked that Ross boy, sent him on his first-ever flying lesson!" she sang, as she danced round with her walking stick, brandishing it like a fencing foil.

Jan and Marie picked themselves up.

"Show over!" sighed Jan. "And I thought we had finally sorted them out! Now it's just as bad as ever. You win one day and you lose for the rest of your life."

"Yes!" said Lady Beddoes, "That's the way of it! Steal and lie and pretend to be nice, but all the time, they're scheming and plotting…" and for a second Lady B was somewhere else entirely.

"But selfish, crabby Beddoes!" She pulled herself up short and peered closely at the state of the children, "Slurry Sister, Broken Boy! Let me see what I can find!" and she reached inside her huge patchwork coat and, with a flourish, produced enough rags to wipe off the worst of the slurry. For once, heavy rain was on their side, washing off some of the stink.

"Now, quick – let the wind push you home – and make a good tale out of it!" advised Lady Beddoes.

"Thank you!" said Marie.

Before she turned away, Lady B looked them in the eyes, as if searching for something.

"Remember that the bull was read down with light from a stranger. Find the light, my little Klečeks!" And with that, she was off again, sword-fighting the wind. Marie felt a question about Lady Beddoes' ancestors swim up to the surface of her mind, but she was too tired even to think about it.

"Are you OK?" Jan asked his sister, putting his arm around her.

"I suppose so..." She shivered, as they dragged themselves away from the deserted farm and back through the lanes. There would be a lot of covering up to do when they finally got home. How could they possibly explain the state they were in? But thankfully, when they arrived back, their mother was out shopping and their father not yet returned from school. They managed to hose down the worst under the outside tap and then they peeled off their clothes and stuffed them in the washing machine. They took turns to bath quickly, and once warm and dry, they were almost presentable by the time Eva came back.

"A car splashed mud all over us on the way home," they said. Eva tut-tutted at mad drivers and Jan and Marie breathed a sigh of relief.

A bit of D.I.Y

Ross was terrified by what might have happened at the slurry pit, and ashamed of running off. After all, it was his parents' farm that the Czech kids had been chased into. But when he came back an hour later, there was no sign of them. What could that mean? He had only meant to scare them. He thought: *They should have known better than to go through the gate. It's their fault they stepped in it. And it's not that deep. I'm sure they managed to climb out. And if he hadn't hit me with the ball in the first place...* But that night, Ross dreamed that Marie and Jan had turned into zombies. They were coming to get him! He woke up screaming for his mum.

The next morning he was pale and jittery – until he saw Jan walking casually into school, large as life. At first he was hugely relieved, but within seconds he was back to his usual sarcastic self. He rubbed the back of his leg where Barmy Beddoes had whacked him.

"It's the Walking Dead!" he sneered at Jan.

"How's it going, mud-man?" giggled a relieved Kerry. Doug was behind them, looking very uncomfortable.

But Ross had made his point. The match was over and he was the winner.

Jan felt terrible. *So this is to be my school life*, he thought. *The stupid ones win and justice doesn't stand a chance.*

***

December could not make up its mind. Great white slush puppies splodged everywhere as they slipped and slid their way into town. The next day the mix of temperature, grey cloud and wind cooked up a huge portion of hail – as if the sky were one huge bean bag cut open. The little white balls bounced and rolled everywhere, knocking on window-panes and hammering roofs. Marie noticed that no one talked about the weather now – they just got through it.

But then came a day that had the perfect consistency – creamy white sky, just above freezing and no wind at all. As the curtains were pulled open at Shoe Cottage, the sky was serving up bowlful after bowlful of snowflakes.

"Delicious!" shouted Marie, as she rushed out to taste the instantly-melting flakes on her tongue. It was a day for winter activities and when Marie arrived early at school, there was already a snowman in one corner of the playground. The younger children were making snow angels and there was a pitched snowball battle which everyone joined in.

In all the flurry, nobody seemed to notice a different sort of fight going on in the corner. Cassie and various 'friends' were holding Kylie down and stuffing snow inside her coat until she began to cry.

"Vot are you doing?" shouted Marie, as she spotted the commotion and ran over.

"Vot! Vot! Full of Snot!" replied Cassie, grinding one more snowball into Kylie's hair, before wandering off laughing.

Too soon the bell rang, and in class Mrs Evans zipped round with the latest writing exercise. Marie's English had improved, but writing a story took all her concentration. Word order was a problem and spelling – well, thank goodness for spellcheckers!

"Wonderful, Marie!" said Mrs Evans, enthusiastically, "I love the idea of a ghostly bull smoking a cigar and driving a big car. You do have a great imagination!"

"You do have a greeeeeat imagination! Vot a vild girl you are!" whispered Cassie, making a face at Marie and imitating her accent as Mrs Evans moved away. Marie stared back at her in total silence until Cassie looked away. But Kylie smiled at her shyly.

"Vot did your mother say?" she asked Ashleigh after lunch.

"Well, I badgered and badgered..."

"Badgered? You have badger?"

"Oh, I mean, I asked and asked and wore her down!" Ashleigh smiled. Ever since the W.I. experience, her mother had done her best to ignore Marie, mostly by avoiding her. However, Ashleigh had come over to play several times, though the invitation was never the other way round...

"Anyhow, I've got my night gear, some cool CDs and warm clothes," Ashleigh went on. "Shoe Cottage needs thick socks!" Marie thought for a second, then got the joke and grinned.

***

The drifts had piled up along the lane as they walked home with Jan. It was like wading through wool and strange to see their boots vanishing beneath the bright, white surface.

"Hello, Mrs K," said Ashleigh, as they wiped their feet on the doormat.

"Ahoy, Ashleigh!" Marie's mother replied and welcomed her into the house. It was Jan's turn to feel excluded, and the moment Ashleigh put on her CD in the living-room and the music began to blare, he made a dash upstairs to his room. Marie felt quite satisfied.

"Boys!" she sighed, and rolled her eyes. The girls

both fell about laughing. Mrs Kleček had made some hot, spiced apple juice and they both sat drying themselves in front of the fire as the snow fell silently beyond the window.

František walked in, brushing the snow from his boots and coat.

"Look at you girls! What a life!" He smiled. "Some of us must work!" And he unwrapped a bundle containing a saw, a cordless drill and a small crowbar borrowed from one of his colleagues.

"Jan!" he shouted and bounded upstairs, after giving his surprised wife a quick kiss. "We have to do something about Marie's room!"

The sound of hammering filtered down, followed by a great cheer. The girls ran upstairs. Marie's floor was covered in black soot, but where there had been plasterboard, there was now a Victorian cast-iron fireplace which had remained untouched and hidden for half a century. "They call it a living-room for a good reason, Marie!" said František, wiping his brow. "You can't go on sleeping there for ever." He began to sweep up the soot with a dustpan and brush.

"I'll go and get some newspaper and kindling," said Jan enthusiastically. And soon the fire was laid and ready to go.

"It's my room, so let me do it!" announced Marie. She grabbed the matches off her father and bent down to light the paper. As the flame caught, instead of curling upwards, the smoke came straight out into the room. Within a few seconds they were all coughing and František had to launch himself into stamping out the fire.

"Blocked!" he exclaimed. "I suppose I'm not surprised. Maybe a bird's nest! We will have to wait until the weekend to look at this properly. Ah well, you girls are definitely sleeping downstairs tonight, after all."

"Here, give me a hand, Jan!" called František, and he pulled a spare mattress out of the landing cupboard and balanced it at the top of the stairs. The living-room was soon turned into one huge bedroom and Mrs Kleček found it hard to squeeze into the kitchen.

"Mmm. Fabuloso!" said Ashleigh as they all squashed around the tiny table and tucked in heartily. "What's Czech for 'delicious'?"

Marie said something that sounded like "Veebornyee!" though the *r* sounded like a rattle of drums.

"Vaybone-yeah!" tried Ashleigh, and Mrs Kleček giggled and gave a little bow.

"*Řízky!*" she explained, pointing at the plate. Mrs K had let the girls join in whacking the pork steaks with a strange, many-pointed hammer until they were flat, then dipping them in an egg yolk and milk mix, and finally coating them in breadcrumbs, before Eva threw them in the sizzling, oily pan.

"It's beats microwave chips any day!" said Ashleigh jealously, as she helped herself to another spoonful of creamy potato salad.

***

Later, curled up on their mattresses, the two girls watched the glow from the fire's embers. The rest of the house was so silent, they could hear the ticking of the kitchen clock.

"Look at that shadow over there," hissed Ashleigh. "It looks like a cobra waiting to… STRIKE!" and she pounced on Marie, slithering and hissing until they both fell back giggling helplessly. The room was warm and sleep felt like a still-far-off visitor.

"I know, what about some spooky stories?" whispered Ashleigh. "I know this great one about the Grey Lady of The Lake, drowned by her evil husband, but still hovering above the water like a kestrel…" She paused. Marie was looking puzzled.

"Vot is smooky stories?"

"S-p-o-o-k-y, you know? Ghosts. *Whooo… whooo…*" and Ashleigh dived under a blanket and flapped her arms around. Marie got the idea and launched excitedly into the Czech tale of the young

woman who tricked bony-fingered Death. Ashleigh shivered, and began her own tale about the Lady Made of Mist.

"And she would hover at the edge of the lake, drawing all the mist into her shape until she was almost solid shadow and then she began to... WHAT was that?" They both jumped, startled by a creaking sound, and turned to see a huge shadow looming down the stairs, creeping straight towards them! They both breathed in sharply at the same time.

"It is only me!" whispered a voice. It was Jan, "Come quickly!" and he pointed upwards.

Marie squeaked breathlessly. "Jan! But why?" Jan put his fingers to his lips and beckoned.

"Come on, then!" Ashleigh jumped up and pulled Marie with her. Without speaking, the three of them crept upstairs and into Marie's room, where Jan closed the door. His torch beam bounced off the walls.

"I was woken by a sort of scratching sound!" Jan explained excitedly. "I think it's inside the chimney. Listen."

Marie and Ashleigh leaned forward. It was faint, but they could definitely hear it too. Ashleigh wished they hadn't just been talking about ghosts.

Marie tried to look more determined than she felt. Ashleigh was impressed and watched as Marie knelt by the grate and pushed her hand into the darkness. Jan steadied the torch, but it couldn't see round corners. Marie felt carefully along the stone. She found something crackly, then hard, then soft. She pulled.

"Oh! It's…" but before she could finish, a great black lump fell out of the chimney. Jan shone the torch into Marie's cupped hands. It was something soft, warm and breathing and it let out a squawk of alarm.

"A jackdaw!" exclaimed Ashleigh. The bird hopped out of her hands and they all chased it round the room until Jan finally caught it, opened the window and let the wind take it.

The bedroom door shuddered open and the light snapped on. František stood blinking and bleary-eyed. "What's going on?" he demanded. "It's sleeping time, not a midnight party!"

"Jan heard a noise and I stuck my arm up the chimney and there was a bird." Marie burbled in Czech.

But František was not listening. "Ježiš-Mankote! For goodness sake! And look at this mess! You can come and clear it up in the morning!" he ordered. "Bed now! I would like some sleep before tomorrow if that is OK with all of you."

The children looked sheepish.

"Sorry, Tatínku!" muttered Jan, and their father ushered them out of the room and closed the door.

The chase is on

In the morning, František slept late and cursed the nocturnal disruption as he tangled himself up in his tie and various duvets on the living-room floor. He banged out of the house, shouting grumpily, "I want that bedroom cleared up before school!"

After breakfast, the children trooped upstairs with damp cloths and a dustpan and brush. Marie pulled open the curtains and the low winter light edged into the room. The jackdaw's nest sat like a huge black lump in the grate, covered in cobwebs and dried-up droppings. But the light picked out something else – a glint of silver.

"Look!" exclaimed Marie.

She pushed the nest out of the way and lifted up the object. She pulled off twigs, leaves and dead spiders and used the cloth to wipe away the soot and dust.

"A shoe!" She frowned, and felt the room go cold.

"A shoe in Shoe Cottage!" laughed Jan.

"Not just any old shoe, either!" Ashleigh said – for, squeezed inside the large, silver-buckled shoe, was a cracked leather pouch. Marie's fingers trembled as she

eased it out. This must
surely hold treasure!
She peered inside.
Paper! Just a thick,
many-folded piece of
paper. Her shoulders
drooped and she sighed.

"Never mind. Let's get on."

"No. Wait." Jan carefully took the paper from her.
"Let's see what it is first." He unfolded it gently. It was
certainly old. There were red wax seals all over it and
the parchment was covered in a thin, flowery,
handwritten script. They took it to the window to get a
better look, but even Ashleigh could not make head or
tail of it. Some of the words were much bigger than
others. Marie could just make out one of them –
Between – and after that a name

"Vin… stead… Bed… does!" she spelt out. Where
had she seen that name before? And what was it that
Lady Beddoes had said when she told them the tale of
the Bagbury Bull? *"It's all in the shoe!"* Marie tried
hard to remember more, but couldn't find the pieces
to fit the puzzle.

"I can't make any sense of this!" sighed Ashleigh,
still turning the paper this way and that. Jan and Marie
looked at each other and shrugged. Their father had
gone and their mother would be no help. So they swept

up the nest and the soot, folded up the paper, and put it with the boot in Jan's rucksack. It was time for school.

***

The salt gritters never came up the lane to Shoe Cottage, and overnight the track had turned to ice. Eva Kleček was certainly not one to let precious baking-trays leave her sight, so some dishonesty and smuggling on the part of the children was involved in liberating one from the kitchen. Jan sneaked out with his coat bulging while Ashleigh was saying thank-you to Mrs Kleček. Once they were out of sight of the cottage, they took it in turns to hurtle downhill, legs in the air and bums on the tray. At the main road, they hid the tray in a hedge and headed into town.

***

No one noticed Kerry hanging back in a doorway. She was standing waiting for Ross when she spotted the children gathered around something further down the alleyway. "Those Kleček kids," she muttered to herself. "Now what are they up to?" She had nothing better to do and there was a little half-wall she could duck behind. Even better, the snow was piled thickly enough to make her approach silent.

"But who's Vinstead Beddoes?" asked Ashleigh, looking at the name that Marie was pointing to.

"He's buried at Hyssington Church," Marie explained, as they huddled around the shoe and its contents. "I saw his name in stone. Then I thought of Lady Beddoes."

Barmy Beddoes! thought Kerry. *That old cow is a danger and a nuisance. How dare she attack my brother... She ought to be locked away!* She peered round the wall to see what the Klečeks and that other kid had got hold of, then she carried on listening.

"The paper must be important, hidden away like that in Shoe Cottage!" said Jan. "Maybe Lady Beddoes can tell us what it means. She would understand this funny writing."

"Okay. Let's meet after school and take it to her," said Marie. "And you, Ashleigh – you vant come too?"

"I wish I could be there, but my Mum's dragging me to the dentist! Let me know what happens!"

***

The sun had just about broken through by lunchtime, as Ross trudged round to the back of Bagbury Hall. He could see his great-uncle leaning over a shovel, scowling. Bob Thomson straightened up as Ross drew nearer and thrust the shovel towards him.

"Ah! Perfect timing! Could do with some strong arms here, lad." Ross looked with distaste down the slimy, foul-smelling hole his uncle was pointing at. "Blocked drain," Bob said. Ross grunted, and started talking as he dug.

"A shoe, eh? And that old wastrel Vinstead Beddoes? Are you sure that's what they said?" Bob looked piercingly at Ross. He was in no mood for any monkeying about.

"Yeah, Uncle Bob! That's what Kerry told me!" Ross wasn't scared of anyone except his great uncle. Bob was just like the weather. You could never be sure what was round the corner. He grimaced at Ross.

"Good lad. You did well. Oh – and I reckon you've sorted the drain too." They both paused to listen to the gurgle of wet sludge finally going where wet sludge ought to go.

"Anyway, they said they're going to Barmy Beddoes' place after school, so she can take a look at it!" Ross was so pleased with himself, he flushed purple.

A chip off the old block, thought Bob proudly. Then he frowned. "I don't like the sound of that! Stealing from my cottage… we'll have to do something, won't we, lad?" He patted Ross on the head and pulled a crumpled fiver from his back pocket. "Now, get on back to school. I'll pick you up at 3.30 sharp.

You'd better be ready!" And Bob stomped off into the house. He didn't even pause at the door to take off his smelly boots.

"First the bracelet, eh, Vinstead! And now this." He looked up at the portrait. "You're just like her, you know – barmy. Hah!" Bob was pacing up and down. "Have you got something up your sleeve that you ain't telling? Eh? Eh?" The portrait stayed silent, though perhaps a faint smirk hovered on its lips. "But you ain't gonna get me this time, oh no!"

***

"Oh no!" cried Marie, as they floundered through the snowy fields after school on their way to Lady B's.

"What now?" said Jan.

"Look, silly *hlupák*!" and Marie pointed up the hill to where a farmer's track ran along its edge. Crouching by the gate was Bob's huge four-wheel drive, headlights shining brightly against the snow, engine softly growling like a beast.

"They're not there to wish us good day!" muttered Jan, as he grabbed Marie and turned to run. But running through the deep snowdrifts was like wading through baked beans. The car had turned through the gate and was ploughing through the snow, pushing it aside as if it were confetti.

How could two children hope to outrun a 3.2-litre turbo-charged metal monster?

"This way!" Marie screamed. She had spotted a deep dip in the valley and a stream. Maybe it would be too steep for the car…

They tumbled downhill through the snow, with the whine of the engine gaining on them every second. Suddenly, they were splashing through the stream and up the other side. Jan took a quick backward glance. The car had paused, as if thinking what to do. Steam poured out of its exhaust and Jan saw that it wasn't just Bob in the car, but Ross and Kerry too, with their faces stuck to the window, grinning wildly as if this was some big game safari.

We're being hunted! Jan thought grimly, but he said nothing. Bob gunned the engine and the car slowly ground down the slope towards the stream.

Jan and Marie scrambled up the hill on the other side towards the safety of the woods a couple of hundred yards ahead of them. Now the car was splashing through the stream below, then lumbering like a tank up the slope behind them. The sound of the engine roared in their ears. The woods were within reach now, but so was the car. There was no other sound in the valley. No birds called, not even a crow. The nearest dark fir trees were only a few steps away when…

"Aieee!" Marie twisted sideways and fell heavily.

Would Bob stop, or would he run them over? Jan didn't wait to find out. He wrenched his sister up and half-carried, half-dragged her into the shadow of the forest where they were invisible. They could hear the car pull up and voices shouting.

"Are you OK?" Jan whispered.

"No… my ankle…" but Marie broke off. The voices seemed to be moving nearer.

"We're coming to get you!" shouted Ross, as he slammed into the trees.

Kerry joined in: "Little thieves, stealing our family stuff!" But it was obvious they had no idea where to look for Jan and Marie. The branches were so dense that no snow had fallen, so there were no footprints to follow. The crashes and curses moved away deeper into the wood.

Jan breathed a sigh of relief. The sounds of the twins grew muffled now that the silent forest was folding over them. When they could hear nothing but their own breathing, Jan decided it was safe to move off.

However, as Marie started to walk, she crumpled sideways with a sharp gasp. The only way she could make progress was by leaning heavily on Jan and using her one good foot. They moved slowly along the edge of the wood, trying not to slip or break twigs underfoot, and keeping far enough in not to be seen from the fields. After half an hour, they were exhausted, wet and hungry. Jan had no idea where they were. The light was failing and the forest grew even gloomier. But Jan could see the path ahead leading on to a main forestry track, with logs piled along the edges.

"Left or right?" he asked Marie. But she was beyond caring. She was shivering badly, her teeth were chattering, and she didn't answer.

"Marie! Marie!" he whispered.

"Tired!" she grumbled. "Want to sleep." Well, he would have to make the decision for them. He turned left, hoping it would lead them out of the woods to somewhere he recognised.

Time for action

The dentist had been a pain. Ashleigh hated fillings, and drilling of any sort filled her with terror, let alone having a needle stuck in her gum too. The dentist, whose manner was sugary-smooth as a lollipop, made some moral point about the evil of sweets as Ashleigh's mouth quietly throbbed.

She was traipsing back along the slush-spattered pavements with her mum when she spotted Lady Beddoes pushing along an old pram. Mrs Jillson made to pull her daughter away from the local idiot. However, Ashleigh was stubbornly rooted and staring at the old woman. Something was not quite right... if she could just take her mind off her mouth for a moment. The bell in the clock tower struck. Of course! What time was it? Ashleigh broke free of her mother's grip and ran over the road.

"Lady Beddoes! Lady Beddoes!" she shouted after the shuffling figure.

"Another one come to laugh? Go away!" Lady B muttered. As she brandished her stick, Ashleigh was tempted to do just that. But she gathered her courage and stood her ground.

"I'm a friend of Jan and Marie! They found a shoe and a paper with the name 'Vinstead Beddoes' on it in Shoe Cottage, and they were coming to see you to find out what it meant!" she said. "Where are they?"

"They never came. I never saw them!" Lady B looked puzzled. But then a remarkable change came over her as Ashleigh's words sunk in. "Paper, what paper? And with Great-grandfather Beddoes' name on it?" A frown ploughed across her face.

Mrs Jillson had had enough. Before Ashleigh could answer, her mother shouted over the road. "You come here right now, Ashleigh Jillson, or there'll be trouble!"

"But Mum, I think there's trouble already!" said Ashleigh, and for once her stubbornness outdid her mother's. She ran back across the road. "Lend us your mobile, please, Mum. I think Jan and Marie might be in danger!"

"Danger! I'll give you danger!" But her mum could see the concern on her daughter's face. The look Barmy Beddoes was giving her from across the road was enough to shrivel anyone, and passers by were starting to take an interest in the proceedings.

"Here!" she said, "And I ain't got many minutes left, so keep it quick!" Ashleigh rang the number, and when Eva Kleček answered, she tried to make herself understood. But all Mrs Kleček kept saying was, "Not here. Not here. At Lady Beddoes." Ashleigh said "Thank you", hung up and handed the phone back. It was getting dark. If Jan and Marie had gone exploring, they would surely have been home by now.

"Lady B, how long have you been out?" she began. But Lady Beddoes didn't seem to be listening. She was sniffing the air like a hound following a scent.

"Wasting time. All this tittle-tattle talk. Been away as long as it takes to trudge down here. No time at all." She whirled her walking stick round. "Goodbye now. Goodbye! Lady B is off to see her old policeman friend!" and with that, she grasped her pram with a determined jolt and set off down the hill towards the local police station.

Ashleigh gazed after her and wondered if P.C. Jim Cheever would believe a word the old woman said.

"Mum, I'll be home in half an hour – don't you worry about me – I need to give Lady B a hand!" And before Mrs Jillson could say anything, her daughter had run off down the road.

**

It was almost like a road – this dark logging track. But instead of leading them out into the countryside, the path seemed to be taking Jan and Marie into the heart of the forest. A full moon hung in the sky like the pupil of an eye, staring coldly down at them. The path was frozen, and Marie was a deadweight slumped against him.

"Come, little Marie, not far now!" he lied encouragingly. But Marie was silent, apart from her laboured breathing. Shoe Cottage might well be a dump, Jan thought, but oh! how he longed for its bright lights and uneven warmth now.

He started. What was that? Not ten yards in front of them, its tail raised in the air, was a fox. Its long,

pointed nose sniffed out for them, but Jan was downwind. "It isn't you they are hunting now!" Jan said softly. He blinked, and the fox was gone as if it had never been there.

***

"There's no way I am going to send my men out on a wild goose chase over the hills on some whim!" sighed Jim Cheever. It had been a long day, and the last thing he needed was this batty old woman and an over-excited girl spinning yarns about ancient shoes and treasure and danger. "I understand your concerns, Lady Beddoes, but in ninety-nine per cent of these cases, the children turn up at home unharmed. In any case, their parents have not reported them missing. They are probably out shopping."

"I've checked all the shops on the high street!" said Lady Beddoes, giving the constable a withering look. "And their mother thinks they are with me – which," she said, opening her huge coat and shaking it vigorously, "they clearly are not!"

"And it's freezing out there – what if one of them has fallen and hurt themselves on the way to visit Lady Beddoes?" Ashleigh exclaimed.

"And if they were there freezing themselves to death while you, Constable Cheever, were sipping your tea at home, glad to be rid of a mad old woman and a troublesome child, how would it sit on your conscience?" Lady B finished fiercely.

Jim scratched the inside of his ear, perhaps hoping he might find some answer in there. "OK, I give in!" he said. "I'll get a couple of the others out with the high beams and four-by-fours and we'll search the land between the town and your..." Jim didn't quite know what to call Lady B's dwelling.

Ashleigh grabbed him by the hand. "Thank you so much, Mr Policeman! You are brilliant!" P.C. Jim Cheever felt his face flush. He rang the Klečeks one more time and got through to František, who had just got back from school. František was trying to sound calm. No, the children had not returned. No, he had no idea where they were – only what his wife had just told him, that they were going to visit Lady Beddoes after school. But they were always back before dark. He was just on his way out now, to see where they were.

Jim promised to keep them informed and put down the receiver. He didn't like the sound of this.

After that, things began to happen. More calls were made, reinforcements summoned, doors slammed, and soon two cars, mounted with searchlights, were standing outside the station ready to go. Jim took Lady B and Ashleigh, while his other two men jumped into the second vehicle. Within a few minutes they were heading up a green lane into the fields. Luckily, the snow had stopped falling. If there were tracks, they would be visible.

***

Jan was confused. As they slowly rounded a corner, he saw a pile of logs he swore were the same he'd seen twenty minutes ago. Maybe they were going round in circles. Maybe the forest was just a series of loops and they would be wandering for ever. But what was worse, was Marie's silence. He knew he had to get her somewhere warm, and quickly. This was all Bob Thomson's fault! What right did he have to scare them like this? And Jan remembered a tale that his grandmother Babi had told him: about the time in 1948 when her cousins had fled for their lives as the Communist Coup took place. It had been snowing then, too. They had escaped through a back window, then driven to the German border, disguised as ski-tourists with only a gold bracelet and a few gold coins strapped round their ankles.

His cousins couldn't even ski, but when you are trying to stay alive, you learn very quickly. Jan knew the story well. A guide had taken them up the ski lift and through some woods, then pointed down the mountain to the German border. And – so high up that there were few soldiers patrolling – they had slipped out of their old life and into a new one.

Babi's stories used to seem like dark fairy tales, thought Jan. But now, he and Marie were lost in the snow and there was no happy ending in sight.

The woods

That night, as Doug walked back from the chippy, he saw the retreating figures of Ashleigh and Lady Beddoes vanishing into his least favourite place in town – the police station. Doug was bothered. Feelings he had never admitted to were knocking on the door demanding to be let in, and Doug couldn't pretend no one was at home. He brushed the snow off and sat down on a wall to eat his chips, by now soggy and rather miserable. He didn't have an appetite and chucked the rest in the bin. He stuffed his hands inside his jacket and began to walk towards the row of ex-council houses at the top of the green lane. Suddenly a police car came rushing past. Doug jumped aside and turned round just in time to see another car roaring up the hill. Without giving himself time to think, Doug took a deep breath and stepped into the the middle of the road.

"What the…!" Jim Cheever slammed the brakes on, and the car slid on the ice, coming to rest a couple of inches from the crazy figure standing right in front of them. In the back, Ashleigh had been jolted hard against Lady Beddoes, although thankfully the seat belt and layers of clothing cushioned her from serious injury. "I might have known it was you, Doug Stretton!" barked Jim, leaning out. "Getting yourself killed might have done all of us a favour!" Clearly, Doug's reputation had preceded him.

"Sorry, P. C. Cheever!" said Doug. Jim didn't know who was more shocked to hear an apology coming from Doug's mouth, himself or Doug. "But I think there's something you oughtta know!" All this do-gooding was beginning to get to him. He broke into a sweat, coughed several times, half-closed his eyes and launched himself into explaining why Jan and Marie needed to be found, and quickly. Jim couldn't believe his ears.

"Get in, quick," he commanded, and Doug found himself squeezed up next to Mrs Beddoes. The blue lights were flashing and sirens blared as the two cars headed for the hills.

The heavy tyres were churning their way up a snow-banked lane when the constable in the front car caught his breath. Two small, glowing points of light were hovering ahead.

"What on earth...?"

Huge and black, as if night had wrapped itself round a ton of flesh and muscle, a bull was charging towards them! And this bull, snorting clouds out of each nostril as it pounded the ground, seemed to know exactly what it was doing. From behind, Jim Cheever saw the front car veer off the track and land floundering in the deep snow, its back tyres squealing. This left the second car like a lone skittle in an alley.

Lady Beddoes was watching, her heart drumming like hoofs. "The bull!" she muttered. "All right, then, dearie! Trying to stop us, eh?" And she motioned Jim to turn left into a gateway to avoid the beast as it thundered down on them. "Stop now!" she commanded, and before Jim could do anything, the old woman leapt out. The bull had turned remarkably gracefully, twirling like a ballet dancer to deal with the second car.

"That's right!" sang Lady B, as if she was coaxing a cat to some milk. "Over here!" She stepped away from the car and with a flourish, pulled out a red scarf that billowed in size until it made a perfect cape.

Ashleigh and Jim swivelled round to see the battle between the old lady of the hills and the bull from nowhere. It was as if her old age had melted away. "Drive forward into the lane!" she shouted, without taking her eyes off the bull, "then open that gate and stand well back." She continued moving slowly down, straight towards the beast. The bull came for her, but she lifted up the cape and all it could stab with its horns was the night air. Frustrated, it turned back, gave

a mighty bellow that echoed across the valley, and charged again.

"Get ready!" shouted Lady B. "You'll need to be quick!" And as the bull made to gore her, she stepped nimbly into the hedge and tossed the cape like a dart, where it clung to the bull's horns. The huge creature careered wildly through the open gateway, thrashing its head from side to side, but it was too late. Jim had swung the gate closed.

"Life in the old girl yet!" Lady B puffed, leaning on the gate, "And you!" she said to the bull, "You won't stop us that easily, Bob! Indeed no!"

Jim was open-mouthed. He immediately dropped all notions of Beddoes being barmy. He wasn't sure exactly what kind of creature she was, but he'd rather meet her than the bull any day, that was for sure.

They both turned, hearing the other car's wheels crunch into gravel and back on to the lane.

***

Jan stopped again to get his breath, sinking down on a log-pile and letting his sister lean against him. Suddenly he heard another sound from further up the track. It rumbled like hoofs. He pulled Marie up again. If only they could make the next corner! He dragged her on. Yes! Yes! And as the path turned, it was as if the forest had finally let go of its grip. For there, bathed in moonlight, lay the snow-wrapped hills, valleys and fields surrounding Priestcastle. Down there was a real world with houses and lights and people. He could see car headlights weaving through the town far below like silent fireflies. He stood entranced.

"We've made it, Marie!" he whispered. "Look!" And something in Marie woke up. She opened her eyes and swooned with relief. But any sense of victory was short-lived. The rumbling behind them grew. Jan had no time to even think about hiding, before the huge, smoking bull bore down on them, fiery lights shining out of its eyes. Jan shielded his face. Marie cried out and fell to her knees. Any second now, and they would be tossed into the air like so many pigeon feathers.

But the roar was switched off like a finger's click. There were several metallic slamming sounds, then footsteps crunching towards them.

"Little prats!" hissed Kerry.

"Shut up!" commanded a voice. Jan looked up at the granite figure of Bob Thomson. It was Bob running the show now, and from his jacket pocket he pulled out something. Ross and Kerry gasped. The eye of the moon reflected on cold silver.

Marie screamed as Bob lunged towards Jan.

Jan made no move to avoid the blow. He didn't cry out. As he closed his eyes, he thought of the fox, who so often outwitted his hunters. There was a soft slicing sound, followed by an awful silence.

"You can't…" squeaked Ross.

"Try not to be as stupid as you look, boy!" Bob turned, with a triumphant look on his face.

Jan opened his eyes. He was still alive. He felt his chest. No blood. He looked up and there was Bob with Jan's bag in his hands, the straps neatly sliced off. The small penknife had served its purpose and now vanished back into Bob's jacket.

"I don't like foreigners. I 'specially don't like clever foreigners who complain," said Bob, gaining momentum as he spoke. "And I hate clever, complaining foreigners who complain about my property and nick my belongings!" As he spoke, he emptied the bag on the ground and held up the shoe.

"Well, Vinstead – I hope I haven't gone to all this trouble just to find your missing shoe!" He laughed as he bent down. "That's more like it!" he said, picking the document up out of the snow.

Jan got his voice back. "My sister is hurt. You've got what you wanted. Help me get her home! Please!"

"Shush! I'm reading!" Under the lights of the vehicle, Bob was carefully studying the document.

***

Two things happened at once. A rampaging gust of wind came out of nowhere, flurrying the snow, causing Ross and Kerry to stumble and Bob to lose his grip on the document. It flew from his hands, and Bob bellowed and began to chase it. A police car appeared out of the forest and another one drew up at the other end of the track, hemming them in.

"Give it back, it's mine!" Bob wailed, his arms flailing. "It's all mine!" In a moment, Jim Cheever was out of the car. He ran to check on the children and ordered the others to get blankets and ring the hospital. Ashleigh had taken off her coat to wrap round Marie.

Ross and Kerry were doing their best to pretend that edging away was a totally natural action.

"Not going for a walk, I hope, Ross and Kerry! Your parents will wonder where you are!" Jim said. The shuffling backwards stopped. "And let me help you, Mr Thomson!" Jim reached up, and somehow the document landed perfectly in his hand.

"So this is what all the fuss is about," he said, and studied it carefully for a few seconds. Lady Beddoes materialised by his side and pointed to part of the document.

Jim smiled. "Well, dear Bob, there's bad deeds – and you'd know plenty about them – and there's good deeds. And this," he said, holding up the ancient document, "is a very good deed indeed."

He began to read aloud:

"By this assent, dated 5th of January, 1891 made between Vinstead Arthur Beddoes of Bagbury Hall and Charles Edward Beddoes of Shoe Cottage of the second part, the dwelling house, estate and land known as Bagbury Manor comprising approximately 215 acres, 6 roods and 11 perches... is hereunto conveyed to the said Charles Edward Beddoes..."

"So Great-grandfather Beddoes actually sold it to Grandad Charles!" said Lady Beddoes, with a smile as welcoming as a daffodil in spring.

"Exactly!" said Jim.

"And that means..." Lady Beddoes was jumping and down on the spot.

"Yes!" It seemed that only P. C. Cheever and Lady Beddoes had a clue what was going on.

Jim continued, "From what I can make out, and with the legal training we plods are required to have these days, I would say that this means exactly what it says on the tin. So, after we've dealt with the charges of harrassment, assault and conspiring to kidnap, it looks like the grand and rightful owner of Bagbury Hall is, after all – our own dear, not-so-barmy Lady Beddoes! She was telling the truth all along!"

Lady Beddoes gave a little bow as Bob Thomson stood, suspended in shock. The fates were truly blowing a big, fat raspberry. And, as the handcuffs closed around him, something fell out of Bob's pocket, glinting gold in the moonlight.

Like a magpie, Lady Beddoes descended on the shining object and held it up. "Dear Bob. After all these years!" It was the bracelet which had been dug up from Shoe Cottage. "But I don't want it. It's just old metal! It means nothing!" and she pushed the bracelet back into his pocket. "Here. You keep it!"

All this time, Jan had been holding on to Marie, while they numbly watched events unfolding in front of them. Now that their ordeal seemed to be over, Marie began crying.

The constable realised action was needed. "We have a child in urgent need of medical attention, and I have a cold cup of tea waiting for me on my desk!" Ross and Kerry were pushed towards the second car to be taken back to the station alongside their great-uncle. Their misery worsened when they spotted Doug in the back of the other car.

"Stab-in-the-back!" mouthed Ross, as they were marched past. Doug wound down the window and grabbed Ross by the hair.

"What did you say? Eh?" The policewoman escorting Ross decided not to intervene.

"Nothing!" whimpered Ross.

"I must have been mad to hang out with you." Doug pulled a bit tighter. "And if you ever roll your

137

eyes at me again, Kerry, or if I ever hear that pathetic sneer of yours, I might think twice about my rule of never hitting a girl!" Ross turned grey. Doug let go and the two were led off.

The moon seemed to agree that the show was over and the clouds rolled over like a final curtain. Within minutes, the battleground where Bob Thomson had met a cringing defeat was no more than a silent patch of snow surrounded by trees.

***

Marie sat wrapped in a blanket sipping hot, sweet tea. The doctor at the cottage hospital had decided that the ankle was merely a bad sprain. Eva and František Kleček had rushed into town the moment they heard the news.

"Maruško, Maruško!" sobbed her mother, coming to give her exhausted daughter a hug. František did not know whether to shout or cry, but as he held his son, he felt that the worst was over.

Digging up the truth

"It all started with Vinstead Beddoes, my great-grandfather," began Lady Beddoes, who was packing up her few belongings scattered throughout the hut. Marie's own stick was parked next to Lady B's, and the two children were curled up together on the sofa. Outside, the sun shone down on the hard, white hills, blasting away all shadows and fears. "Good old Vinstead loved the high life. Bagbury Hall was a place of great activity, with balls and hunts and endless parties that went on from night to morning."

For a second, Marie was transported back in time and could feel the silk and taffeta dress she would have worn as she was twirled round the chandeliered room by a handsome soldier with a devilish moustache…

"But Vinstead was also too fond of his whisky – and when the drink ran through his veins thicker than blood, then his brain grew foggier than any winter morning. His wits were dulled. His inheritance was leaking through his hands. Something had to be done."

Lady B paused for a second to open the door of the stove and give the embers a good poke. "Now,

Bagbury Hall for generations had been passed down, entailed through the male line."

"What is 'entail'?" enquired Jan.

"It means, my dear boy," and a flash of anger flitted across her face, "that only the oldest male son could ever inherit Bagbury Hall, or the oldest male in the bloodline if there were no sons."

Marie looked confused.

"But Vinstead was desperate for money, and so he broke the entail and sold Bagbury Hall and all the estate to his son Charles, my grandad Charlie. This paid off his debts, with some left over for Vinstead to sink and finally drown in his preferred poison."

"But vot has this to do with you?" asked Marie impatiently.

"This my girl, is a legal knot – and it takes time and justice to unravel it. Bagbury Hall is the place I grew up in as a child. It was my home. And my grandfather always said it would be mine one day. You see, he alone knew that Bagbury could now be passed down through the family, and even though I was a girl, and an only child with no brothers, there would be no problem. He kept telling me there was something he would give me when I was older – 'old enough to understand how important it was', he used to say. But that day never came. Before he had time to set his affairs in order, the horrendous winter of 1947 came and the old man gave

in to the 'flu, which killed people in those days. My father Fred was the oldest son. So with his father's death, the estate passed down to him through the male line. However – this is the most important part – knowledge of what Vinstead had done died with my grandfather, and the evidence, the papers that proved the sale, never came to light – until you children happened to go poking about in an old fireplace."

Marie reflected on all the strange comments Lady B had made over the months about shoes and shining lights. What could she really have known?

"Call it an old lady's intuition!" Lady Beddoes spoke as if reading Marie's mind.

"Time passed. I was a young woman – quite pretty,

they used to say!" Jan glanced up, and underneath the wrinkled map of years, he was sure Lady Beddoes was telling the truth. "Many gentlemen came a-courting, including my distant cousin, one Robert Thomson."

"Oh!" gasped Marie, "So you mean... you're Isabella!"

"Yes, child – and Robert gave me that bracelet to convince me of his love. Pah! He wouldn't know love if it slapped him round the face with a blue rose. His eyes were like coins, filled with golden dreams of getting Bagbury. He had never heard of the entail and assumed I would inherit Bagbury and all its wealth at some point. And he was handsome and dashing and charming in those days. I was nearly convinced." Lady Beddoes shook her head, lost in the landscape of memory. "But I turned him down – saw through him. We were out walking, and he handed me the bracelet. But as he dangled it in front of me, I saw his eyes. And they weren't looking straight at me, they were gazing greedily back towards my home! So, I took the bracelet all right. Took it and threw it with all my might... Funny where that bracelet ended up. And do you know the really sad thing? I think that maybe the poor young man believed he had fallen for me. He'd convinced himself... You should have seen his face twist up when I rejected him. He almost foamed at the mouth with rage and I felt frightened of him..."

Jan and Marie were on the edge of their seats. "And vot happened next?"

"My parents died. Cars were just as dangerous then, you know. And there weren't any gritting lorries in the winter then. Up by our strangely-named hill, The Bog, they slid off the road, turned over and were killed." The sadness was carved into Lady Beddoes' frown. "And there I was, eighteen years old, alone in Bagbury, trying to organise a double funeral and run the house and deal with the lawyers – lawyers who then dealt me a second blow. Not only had I lost those I loved, but my home, the place I had grown up in, was snatched from me. After all, I was only a woman!" she thundered, "and Bagbury always went to the oldest surviving male relative. Guess who that was?" And she glowered at the children, daring them to say the name.

"Robert! Bob. Bob Thomson!" they both chorused.

"Oh, yes. And he came up the drive, with my parents just lowered into their graves, smiling such a wicked smile. The fates had spoken and Bagbury was his. I was given one week to pack a few belongings and leave. The town was in uproar, but the new owner was happy to remind anyone who dared speak out that, now that he was landlord of nearly half the town, mouths were better shut. Rents were quickly raised. The friends I was close to in town had to move away. Even worse, no one would take me in for fear of Bob.

I went mad with grief and worry, wandering the hills and shouting at the heavens for letting me down, until I came across this strange little shack, which rather suited the Beggar of Bagbury... So the years passed, my fine dresses turned to rags and memories sank deep into the earth. And here we are now!"

Jan almost stopped breathing, he was so caught up in the tale. But Marie was still not satisfied. "But the deed? The paper ve found?"

"The paper. Ah yes, the deed." sighed Lady Beddoes. "Who knows what devious dreams went through old Vinstead's head? Or maybe it was my grandfather Charlie's sense of humour, hiding the deed in a shoe in Shoe Cottage. But history is full of tales, and sometimes it takes bravery and pluck to uncover them! The deed proves, beyond a shadow of a doubt, that Bagbury is mine. Always was, always will be. And there's not a single thing Bob Thomson can do about it!" Her eyes sparkled as she grabbed both the children and hugged them. "Now, help me pack the kettle and cups away – " and the calm of the story was shattered.

As Jan and Marie left Lady Beddoes' old house in the hills for the last time, she shouted out after them, "Surprise for you at Shoe Cottage! Just you wait!" She gave them a wink, and shuffled back in.

"What was all that about?" Jan asked. But Marie didn't care. Her ankle was throbbing.

"What will we do now?" she asked, as she limped through the snow alongside Jan.

"Go home, I think!"

"Oh great!" Marie had finally got the hang of British sarcasm. Shoe Cottage didn't seem the most appealing destination. However, when they reached the top of the lane, it was to see their parents packing up the car.

"What's happening? Are we going home?" they both asked.

"Even better!" František replied. "We have had a Christmas invitation!" But he wouldn't say anything else. He just smiled when they pressed him with more questions and told them that the quicker they lent a hand, the faster they'd find out! Finally, the lights in the cottage were turned off. The door was closed and locked and the Škoda ground away in first gear down the icy lane.

Shoe Cottage, the keeper of secrets, closed its curtained eyes and went into hibernation.

A tasty revenge

Lady Beddoes was touring the estate that was rightfully hers once more. She strode down a tunnel-like lane that ended with a farm gate. Ross, Kerry and their parents were assembled in the main yard. Their eyes widened as they beheld Lady Beddoes' transformation from bag-lady to woman of means.

"It is always a joy to meet my tenants," she began amiably, "and when they are family, even more so. I have a feeling that Mr Thomson kept our family connection pretty quiet! You will find that, unlike your uncle, I am a reasonable landlady." Ross and Kerry looked daggers at her. *She's a witch*, they thought, *stealing what should be ours one day*. But their dirty looks were scraped off their faces by the force of their new landlady's next words.

"Now, I feel I should inform you that your two children – or should I say infants – thought I was barmy all along and loved to use my little cottage for stone-throwing practice. Perhaps you didn't know?"

Lady Beddoes paused for a second, wondering how venom can jump generations. The boys' parents, Robin and Julie seemed not to have an ounce of malice in their bodies. But Ross and Kerry were beautifully-reproduced miniatures of their great-uncle.

"They spent their time in school and out doing their best to humiliate and bully those nice Czech children Jan and Marie. Now, I'm certain you agree that such behaviour is quite – what shall we say? – anti-social and not the sort that I would like my tenants to display." Robin and Julie were visibly shocked.

Lady Beddoes' voice grew as heavy as rain-clouds. "Of course, it could put your tenancy at risk. So I suggest you curb your children's infantile behaviour!"

As she bid them good day, it was satisfying to see Ross and Kerry grabbed by their ears and pulled towards the dirtiest part of the yard. Their mother's voice rose higher and higher: "First the police! Then the school! And now this! You are double grounded till further notice – no pocket money, no computer, no TV, extra chores on the farm, and you can start by cleaning round the slurry pit!"

Lady B broke into a whistle as she wandered back up the lane.

***

Marie leaned against the hot radiator and looked out at the trees and hills. Then she turned back to look at the big double bed and so much space, you could have fitted most of Shoe Cottage into it. What a bedroom!

Jan came bursting in. "Not bad at all." He looked around. "But hey, my room is smaller than yours!"

"Glad to hear you back to your former whining self!" laughed Marie, and they both headed for the grand stairs that swept down to the ground floor.

"This house needs children to bring it to life!" said the elegant figure who greeted them in the huge hall.

"Lady Beddoes?" asked Marie, hesitantly, wondering if this well-to-do lady in tweed skirt and silk blouse with pearls around her neck could be the rag-ridden Barmy Beddoes of old.

"Of course it's me. And Bagbury Hall is my home!" she declared. "It always was, and thanks to you, it is again. And now it's your home too, for the remainder of your father's job!" The children knew they had been invited for Christmas, but this news was the best present ever. "And by the way, I don't think you'll have any more trouble with certain youthful relations of mine!" she concluded, with a savage twinkle in her eye.

Eva Kleček had taken over in the kitchen. With Lady Beddoes' blessing, she was busy preparing for their traditional Czech Christmas. There was much to do and the children were, for once, happy to be roped into the once-a-year task of making Czech cookies. Great sausages of almond dough were rolled on to the worktop, to be snipped and shaped into tiny, edible crescent moons ready for the oven. But Marie's favourites were the Bear Paws – a mix of dark chocolate, ground hazelnuts, orange peel, cinnamon, butter and flour. The dough was cut into small balls and squashed into buttered metal trays in the shape of animal paws. When this mix began to brown in the oven, the scent filled the house with a delicious incense.

In the grand drawing-room, a huge fir tree from the Bagbury estate tickled the top of the twenty-foot ceiling. It was covered in lights and the base was buried in presents of all shapes and sizes. Jan and Marie had been banned from the room and found it almost impossible to keep from bursting in.

***

The bell rang out and the dining-room doors were opened. Underneath the huge chandelier, the table, long enough for twenty people, was covered in a cloth white as snow. Lady Beddoes had happily taken on the services of Bob's housekeeper Enid. They were cousins, after all... and Enid was now shyly adding the finishing touches to the table. But Lady Beddoes came over and whispered in her ear, "Sterling job, Enid – I hope you've set a place for yourself as well!"

Enid almost cried at the unexpected kindness. For the last forty years, she had never once been allowed to sit down to eat with her brother-in-law. She hurried back to the kitchen to help bring in bowls of steaming soup.

Lady Beddoes sat at the head of the table and looked at the Kleček family.

"I have so much to thank you for, dear friends!" she began. "And you may be wondering how events took such a fast turn. My not-so-dear and, thank goodness, very distant cousin Bob Thomson got his breath back quickly and, after a night in the cells, began to threaten all sorts. However, after his solicitor came and had a quiet word with him, a remarkable change came over the man. According to Jim Cheever, he was still going on about 'that flimsy bit of paper proving nothing!' and saying, 'the law will be on my side!' – although I think we all know about Bob and the law!"

František nodded, thinking of slashed tyres.

"Anyway, his solicitor pointed out that the deed was genuine, and that therefore Bagbury Hall did come down from my grandfather's line to me. There was, of course, the possibility of appeal, but Jim was quite happy to point out all the charges that could and would be laid at his door. With your parents' agreement, my dears, we decided to drop all charges, so long as Bob Thomson left quickly." Lady Beddoes paused,

savouring the moment, before going on to reveal the ace up her silk sleeve. "But though he is a heartless old man, I still have a soul, and could not possibly turn him out into the cold so close to Christmas. So, dear friends," and she raised a glass, "while he finds his feet, or should I say hoofs, I have let the old roarer stay in a little place belonging to the estate – no central heating, somewhat drafty... Sounds familiar?"

Jan and Marie began laughing. "Shoe Cottage!" they shouted in unison. And indeed, for Lady Beddoes it had been a momentous sight to see the puffed-up bully reduced to a shivering shrew as he retreated sullenly from the stolen house with his tail firmly between his legs.

"And as for that bull of his... well, let us just say that that bad-tempered old beast will not be bothering us any more. Instead, let us give thanks for his contribution to the huge steak and kidney pie being prepared for the town feast on New Year's Eve!"

Everyone burst out laughing.

"But enough of the past. Here's to the future!"

They all raised their glasses and drank.

And now, after the earthy fish soup, there would be fried fish and creamy potato salad, followed by vanilla-flavoured sweet moons. Somewhere, a bell would tinkle and although both children knew, as their father slipped out of the room, that it was not really the Spirit of Christmas who had rung the bell, they were willing to suspend belief. And there would be presents, gifts to groan over and be delighted with. And tomorrow, the hills, once closed off with barbed wire and 'Private' signs, would be filled with children soaring and swooping like birds through the snow on sledges and baking-trays.

The only roars would be roars of delight, and the only stampede, that of feet racing back up to the top again.

Czech pronunciation

The language of Czech is filled with quirky pronunciation. Even the word *Czech* is pronounced 'Check'. We put accents on the top of letters which change their sound. The Czech name *Kleček* is pronounced 'Klechek', with a *ch* sound as in 'chat'. The accent ˇ also changes the sound of the letter *s* to *sh*, so *František* is pronounced 'Frantishek'. The letter *c* in the middle or at the end of words is often pronounced with a *ts* sound. *Jan* is pronounced with a *y* to become 'Yan', and *Marie* is pronounced 'Marry', with a slight roll on the *r*.

We are also proud to have one of the most difficult-to-pronounce sounds in the world. It occurs in the family name of our famous composer Antonín Dvořák. The accent above the *r* changes the sound into a partly-rolled *rr* followed by a softened *dge* sound with a hint of *z* in it. It's very difficult to describe – easier when you say it!

Czech glossary

(Pronunciation in italics)

ahoj *(ahoy)*: hello

ano *(anno)*: yes

Bože! Bože! Já mám strach! *(Boray, Boray, ya mam strach)*:
Oh God! Oh God! I am terrified!

Dobrý den *(dobryden)*: Good day, hello

Dobrou noc *(dobrownots)*: Good night

fantastický *(fantastitskee)*: fantastic

hlupák *(hloopack)*: silly fool

Já nerozumím *(yar nayrozzoomeem)*: I do not understand

Ježiš-Maria! *(yeshishmarriaa)*: Jesus and Mary!

koruna *(Korroonah)*: crown – the unit of Czech currency

Maminko/Maminečko *(maminechko)*: Mum (affectionate)

Mankote! *(mankotay)*: For God's sake!

Maruško *(Marrooshko)*: Marie (affectionate)

ne, ne *(nay, nay)*: no, no

Pomoc! *(pomots)*: Help!

řízky *(rizkeee):* pork escalopes

Spi dobře *(spee dobjay)*: Sleep well

Táto/Tatínku *(tahto/tateenkoo)*: Dad (affectionate)

Ty blbče! *(tea blbchay)*: You idiot!

Ty jsi debil! *(tea see debbil)*: Daft idiot!

výborné *(veebornyee)*: delicious

Watch out for more adventures
starring Jan and Marie coming in 2007!

Purple Class
and the Skelington

Sean Taylor

Illustrated by Helen Bate
Cover illustrated by Polly Dunbar

Meet Purple Class – there is Jamal
who often forgets his reading book, Ivette who is the best
in the class at everything, Yasmin who is sick on every
school trip, Jodie who owns a crazy snake called Slinkypants,
Leon who is great at rope-swinging, Shea who knows all
about blood-sucking slugs and Zina who makes a rather
disturbing discovery in the teacher's chair…

Has Mr Wellington died?
Purple Class is sure he must have done when they find
a skeleton sitting in his chair. Is this Mr Wellington's
skelington? What will they say to the school inspector?
Featuring a calamitous cast of classmates,
the adventures of Purple Class will make you
laugh out loud in delight.

ISBN 10: 1-84507-377-0
ISBN 13: 978-1-84507-377-0

Butter-Finger

Bob Cattell and John Agard

Illustrated by Pam Smy

Riccardo Small may not be a great cricketer –
he's only played twice before for *Calypso Cricket Club* –
but he's mad about the game and can tell you
the averages of every West Indies cricketer in history.
His other love is writing calypsos.
Today is Riccardo's chance to make his mark with
Calypso CC against *The Saints*. The game goes
right down to the wire with their captain Natty and
team-mates Bashy and Leo striving for victory, but
then comes the moment that changes
everything for Riccardo…

ISBN 10: 1-84507-376-2
ISBN 13: 978-1-84507-376-3